CW01086275

BOOK MAIL
BY
JASON R. DAVIS

Published by
Jason R. Davis, LLC
Weston, WI 54476

Author's website
http://jasonrdavis.com

Edited by Candace Nola of 360 Editing (a division of Uncomfortably Dark Horror).

Cover Illustration by Jason R. Davis

Dedicated to my fans:

*This book is a love letter to all
of you. The best way I can show
my appreciation is that for each book,
I do my best to continue to scare the
pants off of you. I hope I continue to
do so.*

WARNING:

This book is the most twisted, disturbing piece of fiction I have ever written. This book contains sexual acts that some will find highly disturbing. Please do not read if that may offend you. The end of this book is not for the faint of heart and may offend. I would have issues with this ending, and I wrote it.

PROLOGUE

"Come on!" Lexi snapped at the tripod selfie stick, picking it up from where it fell over. She was trying not to get frustrated, but the damn thing just kept tipping over. How was she ever going to do this if she couldn't figure this out? She was trying to record her first bookflix video, and she couldn't even keep the tripod from falling over.

Lexi had been watching the videos on Flix for a while and she saw more and more influencers going viral; some of them even able to make a living off streaming content all the time. That was what she wanted to do. She wanted to be one of those influencers. She just needed to start making content.

She got the tripod upright. She turned on the light, then opened the camera app and started recording. Here we go. It was time for her first video.

"Hey everyone, Lexi here..."

She paused, not sure what she was going to say. This was her first video. She had to think of something. She needed a catch phrase, something to brand herself with. What though? What was it?

Her mind raced, but she couldn't think of anything.

Crap, well, just start with hello, we'll figure the rest out later.

"Hey bookflix, Lexi here, and I'm new, as you can tell. I love reading books, and well, I want to talk about them. I'm hoping you'll tap that follow button and want to hear about them.

"My favorites are horror books. The grosser the better. I love stuff like Woom, Playground, and what's some other ones... Well, crap, I can't think of them now. The sicker the better, just the kind of thing I love.

"If anyone has any recommendations, just send them my way and I will start reading them. I'd like to start posting reviews by next week, so send whatever you think I would like.

"And I love supporting indie authors. My address is in my bio. Just send some books my way, I'd love to read them. I love some book mail. Remember, book mail is always the best mail.

"Thank you, everyone, and I hope you enjoy my videos. LexiSexy here, telling everyone out there to stay sexy everyone."

She hit the stop record button and let out a breath. She knew she rushed through the video, her nervousness getting the better of her but overall, she felt like she did a great job. Where did that Lexi Sexy come from? She liked it and was amazed how that came off the cuff like that. Maybe she could do this.

Look out world, she was getting started, and she was going to make these videos her bitch.

She just needed to get some books recommended to her so she could start doing some reviews.

CHAPTER 1

Lexi looked at the message she had received, still not sure what to make of it.

"Hey, thank you for the order of my latest book. I see you live in Pekin. I just so happen to be driving into Peoria tomorrow night for a family reunion and can drop off your copy rather than mailing it out. Let me know what you would prefer."

She looked at the message again. Her favorite author was coming into town and was willing to hand-deliver the signed copy of his latest book that she had ordered. She was going to meet him. She couldn't believe it. She was really going to get a chance to meet him, and it wasn't going to be in some stuffy bookstore where she'd have to wait in line for an hour for a quick two-minute hello while he scribbled his name.

No, she would have him all to herself. He would give her the book, sign and make it out to her. She could talk to him, ask him about where he got his ideas from. He wrote masterfully, always in such fine detail, understanding and really pulling her into his character's thoughts.

It was going to be great. All she had to do was say yes. They could meet and he would drop off the book. He would be there, and she would have him all to herself.

Lexi quickly swished over to a different messaging app; this one not associated with her book purchase, and quickly scanned her contacts. She found the smiling, goofy face of her best friend and opened the long ongoing chat session that had existed ever since both had joined the platform.

"*OMG, U R not going to believe it!*" As it was just after one and they had talked only an hour ago, she doubted her friend was asleep. She had barely set down her phone when the screen lit up with a new message.

"*Wat up?*"

Lexi was going to type it out to her friend, but the thought of trying to explain it while she was this excited seemed like too much. Amanda knew who her favorite author was, but to explain that he was on his way to meet her was going to take more than her shaking hands could handle.

Besides, it wasn't like Amanda was a fan of his. She rarely dabbled into the whole Splatterpunk thing, so they weren't really for her. Her taste was more inline with the dark romance craze, which was okay with Lexi, just not her jam.

Had she talked to Amanda about The Demon Seed? That was one of Lexi's favorites. It was about a girl who summoned a demon, but she didn't know anything about circle protection, or any kind of protection, really.

So, when the demon came, it had not only attacked her but had raped and impregnated her with its demon spawn. The child had grown up to be some kind of anti-Christ.

The book itself had been graphic and over the top, but that was what she liked about it. It was one of his newer books and was a lot more twisted than another book he wrote, Witchy Woman. If she was being honest, they were almost the same plot, but Witchy Woman was out of print, so maybe he had rewritten it, and re-released it? Who knows, and truly only hardcore fans like her would have even heard of the older book.

"*Come on, wat the scoop?*" Lexi saw her phone light up again with the new message. Lexi ignored her friend's message and switched back to the shopping app where she'd purchased Skulz's latest release. She saw the thumbnail of the book she was excited to read, the dark background with a large mailbox in the center, the word 'BookMail' scratched above it, which was the title. She opened the message she had received from the author and clicked on the u-turn shaped icon. The reply window opened, and she typed her message.

* * * *

Lexi pulled into the well-lit parking lot of the large department store, a little self-conscious of no other cars being there. She knew it made sense; the store had closed hours earlier, and it was late.

There was nothing to worry about, right? This guy was a famous author, not some creep she had found on a dating site. She had already bought the book and told him who to make it out to, so he was just dropping it off and then heading to his hotel. He was only in town for a family reunion, so it was a coincidence that he was even there. Meeting him there just saved them both on shipping and she got to meet him. How cool was that...?

It was extremely cool.

So why did the butterflies fluttering in her stomach make her feel like they were eating her on the inside?

Probably because she had spent the last twenty-four hours being berated by Amanda, telling her she was being a moron for meeting some guy she didn't know in the middle of the night. This was getting kidnapped 101. Lexi was doing all the things she shouldn't be doing.

Yet here she was with Amanda, not talking to her, and so far, nothing to prove her friend wrong.

She parked in the center of the lot where it was the brightest. Her car was turned so that she could see any cars coming in and out of the parking lot. Just because she wasn't worried about Skulz trying to do anything, it didn't mean the rest of the world was safe. This was Peoria after all, and crime had only been getting worse every year. Every day she heard there were more and more shootings.

And why couldn't you meet him in the morning? He was busy; he had a full day tomorrow. This was just easier for him to stop by on his way to the hotel. The department store was right off Route 6 and the hotel was a half mile down Knoxville Ave. This was just a quick pit stop for him, and she was the one getting to meet him and get the signed book. It made sense that she inconvenienced herself.

She listened as the night quieted around her until the droning of the cars on the nearby highway became a lullaby of white noise. She could feel herself struggling to keep her eyes open as the constant hum of the traffic kept weighing down her eyelids, ready to pull her into sleep.

Yeah, he's going to show up and I'll be asleep and miss him.

Lexi tried to keep her eyes open, but time passed. She could feel herself drifting off.

Until something pounded on her driver's side window.

Her eyes shot open, and she pulled herself up in her seat. Her breath caught in her throat, joined by her heart, that was trying to escape. She had slipped down as she had been drifting off, but now was upright. If she'd been any taller, she'd have hit the steering wheel, but for once her short legs were a good thing. She felt like a klutz as she worked to remember how to roll down the window, then after trying to do so, realized that with the car off, there was no power for it to go down. She reached for the handle to open the door, but realizing she'd push him back with the door if she tried to open it, she reached for the ignition to start the car to lower the window.

And what if it wasn't him? What if it was some random stranger?

All of that seemed like it happened in a fraction of a second as her mind struggled to pull free from her previous slumber. As it did, she realized just how bad it had to have looked. She could feel the heat rising to her cheeks and felt that right there, she was going to die of embarrassment.

Lexi, you are such an idiot!

"Sorry, didn't mean to wake you. Are you Lexi?"

Lexi looked out her window at the tall, older guy who stood outside. It was hard to see him as the damn light was behind him, darkening all his features. She could just make out his scruffy beard and glasses, but she was fairly sure this was Jacob Skulz. It looked like he had the right build, but the rest was lost to shadow.

He looked scummier than she would have expected. While the black and grey beard was never well kept in his book jacket photo, the man looking down at her was a dogged mess. Not only was his hair all over the place, he wore an old, laundry faded black shirt that had some old metal band on the front. MEGA- something. She couldn't quite make it out. There were holes in the fabric, and it looked like it hung off him like it was two sizes too big for his frame.

If this man hadn't said her name, her first thought would have been that this was some random homeless person who happened on her in her car. She still wasn't entirely certain it wasn't. Maybe this was someone who knew her from somewhere and that was how he got her name.

This is a mistake. You should never have agreed to this. Don't get out of the car. Don't you dare.

Lexi caught herself from reaching for the door handle, no longer sure about any of this, but let it hang over the lock button instead. Had she locked the car when she'd first parked? She tried to remember. She had a hard enough time locking it when she went into the store, something Amanda had criticized her for many times in the past. Remembering to lock it when she'd parked and was sitting inside of it, she had no clue. Maybe?

He must have noticed her reluctance as he nodded and backed away from the car, raising his hands as he did.

"Sorry, didn't mean to frighten you. I was supposed to meet someone here. Really. I guess I was mistaken." Skulz said as he turned and was walking back to what she assumed was his car. He must have pulled in while she had drifted off and missed him coming into the lot. He was parked a few spots away, just on the edge of the pool of light from the overhead lamp.

Damn, it really is him. What are you thinking? He just had a long drive. Of course, he doesn't look as well-groomed as his publicity photo. How well do you think you look before your first cup of coffee and a chance to put on makeup?

She pushed open the door and slid out of the car.

"Mr. Skulz?" Lexi called out. He had just reached his car, and she could hear his key slide into the door. That was when she took notice of the old vehicle. It was a large, box shaped automobile that looked like a dinosaur in the land of time forgotten. It was rusted in various places that finished the sparkling red that almost flowed in the little reflection of light it caught. She thought it was an Oldsmobile or a Buick (were they the same thing?). She didn't know much about cars. Especially old ones like that.

Slowly, the older man turned around to face her. She could see him a little better, and it caught her off guard. His t-shirt and regular everyday looking blue jeans stood out as strange in the early August heat. His face was sunburned to a bright red, as though he'd been outside all day and his hair was windblown, allowing the scar that ran along his forehead to be clearly seen.

She didn't remember that in his photo, though she guessed it could have been recent or photoshopped.

10

"Lexi?"

Was she really doing this? *Lexi, just get back in your car. No book was worth risking your life.*

She wanted to argue with herself, but all of her agreed this was a really dumb idea. Which is why it surprised her when the words escaped her. This was incredibly stupid, yet she just couldn't stop herself from doing it. This... this was why she was always dating the wrong types of people.

"Yeah, that's me."

"Ah, good. Thought I may have come across someone homeless and that you'd already left. Sorry for being so late. It was a long drive down from Wisconsin and my bladder doesn't hold up like it used to."

"Sorry to hear that."

"Is what it is."

He stayed by his car, not making any movement to get closer to her. He seemed just as uncomfortable as she did, looking around at the empty lot as he fidgeted with his hands.

Maybe he was just as afraid of her as she was of him?

He looked down at them as though noticing for the first time what he was doing and put them in his pockets before looking up at her. He forced a weak smile.

"Sorry. Usually not one for meeting new people. I like to stay pretty private. I'm kinda a hermit that way."

"Oh, I get it. I'm the same way. I usually only talk to my best friend."

"Oh, she here too? You didn't come alone, did you?" He craned his neck, looking around her. She supposed he was trying to see into her car, but he quickly gave up to look around at the empty lot, again scanning to make sure no one was there.

"Yeah, just stupid ol' me. She wasn't happy that I came. She's not currently talking to me."

"Sorry to hear that," he said, but she didn't get the sense that he cared at all. "So, I got your book. I signed it before I left, so it should be good to go."

He was talking as he opened the back car door and reached in. He pulled out a shopping bag wrapped around a rectangular object; the cover of the book was just barely visible through the thin plastic.

Lexi walked over to him, excited to have and hold the new book. Before she realized what she was doing, she snatched it out of his hands, even surprising the older man.

"Woah," he said as he took a step back from her, quickly scanning the area, looking for anyone who might be ready to jump him.

"Sorry. I just love your books and can't wait to read this one."

"Oh, going to start right now?" He was watching her as she studied the bag.

"Oh no, I gotta Flix my reveal of it first. You don't mind, do you?"

Lexi was already pulling out her phone from her hip pocket in her shorts.

"I'd rather not. Sorry."

"Oh." The disappointment was clear in her voice, and she fought herself from giving him her pouty face. She didn't think he would go for it, no matter how well it did with her followers. "Okay then."

"I hope you like it."

"I'm sure I will. I love all your books."

"Oh, which one's your favorite?"

"The Demon Seed."

"Really? Huh. I wouldn't have guessed that."

"No?"

"Not really. What happened to the main character in that one was brutal. I didn't see you being into that type of thing."

Lexi could feel her cheeks turning red as she became flustered, realizing what he'd just said.

"Oh, no, I'm not into that type of thing, you know. I just liked the characters and how scary you made it. Oh no, I'd never want to be- you know."

"Sure," he said as he gave her a smirk that told her he didn't believe her.

"Thank you for the book," Lexi said, starting to back away towards her car, suddenly self-conscious and no longer wanting to spend time alone with the man smiling at her. There was something off about him. She noticed for the first time that he was wearing gloves, and he kept watching her as she backed away.

She bumped into her car, not realizing she was that close to it. She briefly looked, checking that it was her car and not someone else's, having magically arrived in the empty parking lot. Then she turned and opened the door, climbing in with only briefly taking her eyes off of him.

She waited until he was in his car, then watched as his lights came on and the car was heading toward the exit before she looked at the bag. It was time for the unboxing video. Not that this was going to be a good one filmed in her car, but she couldn't wait. It was a new Skulz novel. It was given to her by the author himself. She just wanted to squeal.

She grabbed her necklace phone mount and put it over her head so that she could be hands free while recording. Not that it was actually called a necklace mount, but it was what she thought of it as, as the round piece of metal wore like a necklace around her neck, but it was solid and on one side of it, a magnetic phone mount. The design worked so she could look down and have her hands free while unboxing products people sent to her to promote on her Flix page. It looked unflattering, but no one would ever see the behind the scenes of her wearing it.

"There we go," Lexi said to herself once the phone clicked into place. She couldn't help it. She was so excited as she opened her camera app and started recording.

She held up the bag so that it was visible in the video, the light overhead giving it a nice ambiance. She just wished she could do something about her steering wheel. It made for a terrible background.

She looked around the parking lot, and not seeing anyone, got out of her car.

The out-of-focus blacktop of the lot was much better, she realized as she held up the bag again, getting it into frame.

"Hey, everyone. LexiSexy here, Flix fam, and guess what I have? I have the latest Jacob Skulz novel, and it was just given to me by the author himself. Sure, did I just travel to a spooky parking lot in the middle of the night and meet someone I didn't know? You're damn right, I did. You know how you would get me into the back of the van? No candy for this girl! I just need books!"

Lexi added a little flair by shaking the bag in her hands and figured when she actually posted the video later, she'd add spooky caption font to it to make it more visually appealing.

"Okay, so are we ready?" Lexi pulled the wrapped book out of the bag, letting the plastic bag drop to the ground. She paused for a moment, confused at the black wrap around the book. It looked nice, but she could've sworn she'd seen the cover when he'd first presented it to her. Must have been her excitement playing tricks with her.

"I'll pick that up later. Don't worry everyone, I'm not a litter bug, but okay, so we have the book wrapped in what looks like black tissue paper. So festive. Nice and creepy, right?"

Lexi ripped open the paper until she had the book in her hands.

"Here it is. His latest book. Cool title," she said as she read 'A book to die for...' on the front. She turned the book over, studying it, showing it to the camera.

As she did, she noticed that there was something sticky on the cover. She pulled her hand away from it, looking at her fingers. There was some kind of residue on them. She sniffed it but couldn't place the acrid smell. She wasn't about to taste it.

She needed to wrap up her video, but she suddenly felt very tired. The world around her grew unsteady. She wobbled, and not intending to, fell back against her car to use it as support.

"I don't feel right. Guys. I don't think LexiSexy is okay."

Lexi saw a pair of glowing white eyes floating in the parking lot.

"I know you. Don't I?" she said to the red car as it pulled up. Lexi tried to open her own car door, sensing that she needed to get back in there. But why? It was hard to think of anything. It was like simple words and thoughts spun just out of her grasp as she struggled keep her eyes open. Her eyelids fluttered while trying to do so, but they just grew heavier, becoming a weight she couldn't lift.

She found herself lying on the ground, not sure how she'd gotten there. There was a pair of shoes in front of her and it was getting dark. No, it wasn't, but someone was blocking the light.

"Hello, someone."

She wasn't sure if she only thought of saying it or if she'd actually said it.

"This one seems like she's got a lot of spunk," a low, growling voice rumbled. "This should be fun."

"Shush. I told you I got this one. Though I think you're right. She'll make an excellent MC."

She heard voices. She thought she recognized one of them, but thoughts refused to form through the fog that grew more intense. She could feel her mouth opening and

15

closing but wasn't sure if words escaped her. Everything felt alien to her. Distant, like she was falling into her own mind, a prison that she couldn't escape to regain control.

"For someone who said they've read all my books, I really am surprised you'd meet me in an empty parking lot."

Lexi never had a chance to respond before she slipped into sleep, the drugs taking over.

CHAPTER 2

"Damn it L, call me back? He didn't dump you in a ditch and rape you, did he?" Amanda disconnected the call, frustrated that she'd just left her thirteenth voicemail. She was done with her first class of the day and was rushing to her car. She had to be at work in half an hour, so that night she could come back to the junior college in time for her night class. Thursdays sucked as she had the long break in the middle of the day. Her boss knew she was available and needed the money. She was a college kid paying her own way. She needed all the money she could get.

At least it was close to the end of her summer semester, and she would have a few weeks of break until fall semester started.

Though as much as she needed the money, she thought about calling in. This was not like Lexi.

Amanda checked her friend's Flix page again and still no new posts. Something else that was out of the ordinary, as her friend always posted. Her favorite foods, books, you name it, Lexi posted about it. She was convinced she was going to become one of those famed influencers, so she wouldn't have to get a real job.

Amanda didn't think having to post videos all day was all that illustrious, nor was it easy, but Lexi had it glorified that it was her thing, the way she'd become a celebrity after living in such a crap city like Peoria.

At least Lexi knew what she wanted. You're still burning the candle at both ends, working and going to school full time while you can't decide what you want to do when you're done.

Which was true for now. She was leaning towards going into English Education. She liked to write, but wasn't that good at it. She could learn more about it and if becoming a writer didn't work out, she could teach as a backup. The only thing holding her up from doing so was that she wasn't good with kids and didn't think she would make a good teacher. It wasn't her passion.

She got into her car, again disgusted by not being able to decide just what she wanted to do. Dammit, why did she have to make all these plans and figure out everything now? As her mom liked to tell her, her whole future was tied up in this decision.

Nope, not going to think about them, Amanda chided herself, as she was again losing her train of thought. It was hard. She was worried about Lexi, but didn't know what to do. If she hadn't gone off to meet some stranger last night, Amanda would have just thought Lexi stayed up too late and slept in. Amanda wouldn't even be checking in on her.

But she had met a stranger... Where did she go to meet him?

Amanda tried to remember and eventually she had to scroll through her messages to find it.

Well... that was on her way to work. She doubted she would find anything, but she could at least drive by there.

First, she called in, letting her boss know she was running late. Sam didn't care too much. It wasn't busy yet, but if she missed the lunch rush, then they would have problems.

She called Lexi's number again. The phone continued to ring...

MISSING PERSONS: LEXI PEABODY
VIDEO EXCERPT

Hey Flix fam! LexiSexyReads back again and ready to kick off this spooky season with another spooktacular horror rec. I told you last month about this indie author that I'm getting into, Jacob Skulz. Well, I bought another one of his books and this one delivers some mischievous, witchy fun. It is definitely the right book to get me excited for Halloween.

And is it too early to celebrate? Oh, it's never too early for Halloween. See, as soon as the first Spirit store opens in September, it is time, and girl, ours opened yesterday.

So, Witchy Woman, written by Jacob Skulz. Very interesting book, and not a long read, which I liked. This is a one-day book, but don't get me wrong, it was gory and heart wrenching. Definitely a twofer.

The story follows Mabel, a woman with a broken heart after her boyfriend slash fiancé, decided he didn't want to have kids and Mabel was, you guessed it, pregnant. You already hate the guy for leaving that way, but as it goes on, you find out that he's been abusive towards her and has played games with her from the moment she moved into his place. Now he's breaking up with her, and she is broke, pregnant and has nowhere to go.

She ends up getting kidnapped off the street when she was trying to just hide from the world and is taken to this creepy guy's house, where she's locked away in a room full of books, which was really weird. The guy has her locked up, but he's strangely nice to her. He almost becomes protective of her and is keeping her well-fed. It's a real mind trip.

But she still can't leave that room except for using the bathroom.

So, in this library where she is locked away, there are all these books on witchcraft, Wicca, devil worship, all these different paganistic principles, and for the witches in the audience, I do understand that there is a difference between Wicca and satanism. The author knows that as well and does a good job making sure there is a clear distinction. Which is good because things go dark, fast.

Mabel figured out that this guy kidnapped her because he wants to sacrifice her baby once it is born, so she starts teaching herself from these books. She learns how to summon a demon as she wants to summon one and have it kill her kidnapper.

I'm not going to tell you more about what happened after she summons one of the foulest demons from hell. That you'll have to find out for yourself.

Now I'd tell you that you need to go out and get a copy of this book to read, but this is not easy to find. From what I researched, this is the only Skulz book out of print, and it does mark a transition from his earlier works that were more about the evil inherently in people, this marks the first book where a demon was a part of the story.

Now, while I love this writer, I will say from what I've read, he does go hard into demonology in almost all his books after this one. Almost makes you wonder what happened to him to bring on the change. Either way, the more I read, the more Jacob Skulz has become this girl's favorite author.

Until next time, creeps. Stay sexy.

CHAPTER 3

The first thing Lexi felt was the pain shooting through her head, making it near impossible to think. As her awareness grew and she felt herself emerging from the fog of sleep, she felt a wrongness for how she sat. Her head felt like it was a massive weight slumped forward in an awkward position. She couldn't lift it; the effort too much, and there was a stabbing kink of pain in her neck when she tried.

Now lightning bolts of pain shot through her body to her toes, curling them as her head stayed locked in the unnatural position. She didn't feel like anything was restraining her; it was her own body working against her. The pain in her neck tried to dominate the pain shooting through her head but lost as the pounding grew worse, coursing up the back and throbbing as though her skull was ready to explode.

Wetness ran the length of her cheeks, and she knew without opening her eyes she was crying. Her eyes felt crusted over, and she wasn't ready to open them yet. She didn't know if she wanted to as she slowly recalled what had happened before she'd passed out: the meeting, the book, the sticky cover... and then the stench of his coffee, smoke heavy breath as he lifted her up, probably to put her in the trunk of that huge car of his.

"Oh, you're going to be such a great character in my next book." She had heard him say it as he closed the trunk lid. "So naïve, meeting a stranger in a parking lot. You made this so simple. Really, what were you thinking?"

Had she dreamt that? She wasn't sure. She remembered slipping into unconsciousness, but there were other memories of when she thought she was asleep. Memories of her in the dark trunk, bad roads as she rocked and rolled around as he stopped here and there. A sense that there was a presence in there with her; the feeling that something warm occasionally pressed up against her, a slithering feeling as though something wormed its way up her legs...

It was all a jumble and much of it, she wasn't sure if it was a dream or if she had partially woken up.

She vaguely remembered being dragged somewhere, but hadn't had the wakefulness to open her eyes and see where she was. She was tossed somewhere, put into a chair and felt her arms and chest getting tied to it.

That was the last thing she remembered before time slipped away again. She had no idea how long she'd been there.

Lexi tried to raise her right arm and, though she barely had the energy to lift it, could feel the pull of the restraint tight on her wrist. Even if she had the strength, she would never be able to get up from wherever she was.

As more of her senses awakened, she could smell the stench of her surroundings. Urine, shit, and rotten meat all attacked her senses, and she felt the rising bile only seconds before it erupted from her, the warmth of it showering down the front of her shirt.

A shirt. She could feel the cloth become sticky on her chest. At least she was wearing a shirt.

She wasn't sure why, with her sitting there in her own vomit, probably piss as well considering the smell and warmth between her legs, that the knowledge she was still clothed allowed her some semblance of relief. It was enough that she could bring herself to open her eyes.

22

Initially they were crusted shut, and it took effort to get them fluttering to work free some of the eye gunk that was caught in her lashes. It was a fight, but she finally got them partway open. The world was still dark, and she was filled with the sensation that there were pieces of crud in her eye touching her pupil. She struggled with the urge to reach up and clear away the nasties, but all she could do was flutter her eyes.

She finally got her eyes open enough to take in that she was in a room, at least what she could see of one. She was sitting in a chair, a dim bulb overhead, and in front of her, roughly five feet away, was a large, red door. The surrounding wall was black, like the walls of the rest of the room, as much as she could see.

She kept trying to lift her head, twisting it as she did as the kink continued to hold it down. She heard and felt the popping in her neck. It was stiff and sore because she had been unconscious for who knew how long and in that time her head had been dangling, resting on her chest in one of the most uncomfortable positions to sleep in. The most intense part of the pain was towards the back of her neck and she felt like something was jabbing into the right side just between her neck and ear. Her instinct was to reach back there to try to massage away the pain, but was reminded again that her arm was immobile.

That little bit of relief she had felt just moments before was quickly vanishing as she struggled with such a basic thing as lifting her own head.

"Fuck!" she screamed, feeling the scratchiness of her throat.

"Help!" she cried out, shouting as loud as she could, trying to put all the energy she could muster into that one loud scream. She needed to put everything into it because who knew how long she would be able to yell. "Please someone, help me!"

She screamed, wailing, until her throat burned, and she felt her neck grow tired from all the effort of both holding up her head and yelling as she had. It was a struggle to keep herself sitting there. She couldn't remember a time she'd ever felt as physically drained as she was and wanted nothing more than to collapse in upon herself.

"Help me, please." She spoke this last one as the sobs overwhelmed her.

Nothing happened. Her shouts seemed to be absorbed by the walls.

Her head still felt like a hundred-pound weight on her shoulders, but she was finally able to lift it, her neck sore from the exertion. At least now she could look around. She took in more of her surroundings and noticed the dark, odd shapes that jutted out, covering all the surfaces of the tiny room she was in. They were like dark cones poking out. Whatever they were, they seemed to be making this room quieter than she would think possible, as she couldn't hear her voice echoing off the walls when she screamed.

It truly was hopeless. No one was going to be able to hear her. No one was going to be able to save her.

She looked away from the walls, as they were nothing but a source of more frustration.

How could you have been so stupid? Who does that? Who meets a stranger in the middle of a department store parking lot in the middle of the night? How dumb could you be, and for what? You were just going to get a new book. Really? All this was because you didn't want to pay for shipping, and you wanted to meet the author. So how did that go for you?

That was when Lexi noticed the whitish colored objects below her. She knew what they were and felt her stomach twist. They were scattered on the floor in front of her and collected around her feet. Some were obviously dead animals; dogs, possible raccoons or squirrels, but there were larger ones, too. Bones that looked too similar to her own scrawny arms. She looked at the metal door in front of her, trying to avoid the grisly sight at her feet. Lexi wasn't sure how she had first seen it as bright red. She glared at the large, brown door looming in front of her, an insurmountable barrier that held her from her freedom. It looked ancient, almost sealed in the frame, permanently trapping her there. Rust speckled along long scratches where desperation had won out over sanity and people tried to claw their way through the solid door.

Lexi hoped she never got to that point. There was no way she would ever be able to get through it, especially as there was no handle or keyhole on her side. There was nothing that she could grab onto to pull it open.

Frustration dropped her gaze back to the graveyard of bones around her. She hadn't noticed before what was placed next to the door. They had to have been put there, and it must have been a sick reminder that somewhere Skulz was probably watching her because at the base of the wall was a row of human skulls. They were all turned to look at her; their lower jaws missing so that the top row of teeth held in skeleton smiles. They were angled up so those eyeless sockets could watch her as she was stranded there.

She counted five of them. There had once been five other people; all of which had probably died there in the same room as her. They had all been trapped, just as she was, and none of them lived. They had probably been smarter than her and hadn't survived. They were all dead, and she was going to be next.

She heard the loud clank from the door as a heavy lock shifted. Then the door scraped across the floor as it slowly opened.

CHAPTER 4

She recognized him the moment his large head peeked around the edge of the door. He looked at her, and his eyes bulged wide, as though shocked to see her looking back at him. He whimpered briefly and went away, slamming the door. A second later, she heard the lock reengage.

She couldn't stop her rapid breathing and this time she knew it was piss that was warming her thighs. Adrenaline was shooting through her, and she felt some of her strength returning as she pulled against her restraints. Frantic, she tugged at them in a sudden burst of anger infused terror racing through her.

"Ahh, let me out of here, you psycho!"

She pulled at her restraints, both trying to kick out her legs and pull with her arms. She wasn't able to break free. Instead, she was out of breath and tired.

Fresh tears escaped, running down her cheek, and she couldn't stop the sobs that followed.

She was lost in despair when she heard him. She looked up to see him standing there, though he seemed different from when she'd met him. His shoulders were scrunched in; his gaze downcast as his head hung low. If she didn't know better, she would never have thought this guy could hurt anyone. He was standing by the wall with the line of skulls at his feet that clearly said otherwise.

"I'm...I'm sorry. He shouldn't have brought you here," Jacob Skulz, her abductor, said.

Lexi continued to sob, not looking up at him, shying away as he kept his own eyes downward.

"He does this. I'm so sorry. You shouldn't be here."

"Let me go," Lexi said, barely able to get the words out. "Please."

"I can't. He wouldn't like it if I did that. He'd be mad at me."

Lexi let out a fresh wave of tears, fighting to control them. They just kept coming. She didn't want to be this way. She wanted to scream at him, but her thoughts kept going back to first meeting him. How stupid could she be? This was all her fault, and she deserved this. She was the dumbest person on the planet. She went against everything her mother, friends or any other woman out there would have told her was a wise thing to do. She deserved this.

The thoughts kept repeating. Even as she tried to convince herself that they weren't true, her sobbing wouldn't stop. It was hard for her to process what he had just said as new tears came, followed by her own anger with herself. This was all her fault.

What had he said?

"He who? Who will be mad?"

"Him!" the man standing there exclaimed, almost pleading with her to understand. "You met him last night. He brought you here. He would be very upset with me if I let you go. He brings characters here for his books. He wants to write you. You're going to be a character."

Lexi could feel her chest seize and she just wanted to lift her arms to hold herself. To curl herself up into a ball and push herself back into the corner. She closed her eyes so she couldn't see him and sniffled back some of the mucus that was running down her face, mixing with the river stream of tears as she tried to keep what little composure she had.

"I met with you last night. You brought me here."

28

"No, it was him. I don't like it when he brings them back here. I don't like it when he hurts them. I wish he would stop. I just want him to stop."

She could hear him pounding his head against the metal door, but she kept her eyes closed. It was easier. She found she was starting to catch some of her breath and if she focused on it, the sobs no longer ripped through her as violently.

"Stop it. I saw you. You brought me here. Just stop it. Please. Let me go. Let me go and you can do your sick, whatever this shit is to someone else. Why do you even want me, anyway? I was a fan. I liked your books. I bought them, I read them. Why me?"

"It wasn't me. It's him. He likes the fans. I try to stop him. He won't. He likes to-"

The man went silent. Lexi sat there, sniffling back the last of her running sinuses. After a time, she opened her eyes and looked up, sure that he had somehow silently slipped out, though she didn't know how with the scratching the door makes when it's opened.

He was still standing there, holding himself with his head bowed. It looked like he was sobbing, but she didn't see any tears. No, was he whimpering? The man was whimpering as he stood there, not making any move to go.

"He likes to test things for his books. He says fans are the easiest to get, so he brings them back here. Then he... then he-"

The man never finished as his sobs worsened as he fell back against the wall. She watched as his legs gave out and he crashed to the floor, sending the skulls clattering along the tops of other skeletons.

Lexi was watching him, unsure what to say. She sat in her own piss. She was still tied there, and what? Was she supposed to feel sorry for this man? What kind of game was he playing?

29

Though some part of her did question if something was wrong with him? Did he have split personalities? Was that an actual thing outside of movies?

Well, of course, it had to be a thing. Otherwise, they wouldn't get away with using it.

Was he sick?

If he was, maybe she could use that.

Lexi looked at the man that was curling up into a ball. He was pushing away the bones that surrounded him and they scraped along the floor.

"You can let me go. We can end all of this. He doesn't have to know. Please." Lexi was working through her own tears, fighting against the shutdown that kept wanting to own her and make her into the damsel in distress. Lexi always hated that trope, and she was fighting from turning into one herself.

"Nope. Fuck it. This isn't working for me." The man on the floor suddenly exclaimed as he quickly got to his feet. He stood and wiped away the grime and bone dust, though he must not have been able to get them clean enough, as he bent forward and wiped his hands on her shirtsleeve.

Lexi felt her breath catch in her lungs and she tried to recoil from his touch. She had nowhere to go. She couldn't stop him from touching her. She tried to back away from him as far as she could in her own skin, holding her breath until he finally backed away, and she let it out. She wanted to let it out slowly, but it came out in a scream mixed with uncontrollable shaking as she tried to push away the sensation of having his hands on her.

A fresh wave of tears brought on a new clutching at herself even if it was only in her mind. She closed her eyes and felt her lip quivering as she wanted to speak but couldn't find the strength to form words. Even if she could, she didn't know what to say. She could sense that he was standing there watching her, looking down at her.

"The split personality thing wasn't working for me. It's been done so many times. Though really, James McAvoy did it best and after that, why even try? No. No, I don't think that's where this story is going. Don't you agree?"

"What- what do you want from me?"

"Oh, I think it's too soon for that. Much too soon. We don't even have a story yet. We're just getting started, and this is only the beginning." She looked up and saw the spark in his eyes. He was ecstatic, and she watched as he was getting fired up.

As he was talking, something that he said before was irking her, trying to get her attention. What was it she was missing? He said something, and as he spoke, she felt like it had been right there. There was something she missed before.

He was talking about this being the beginning of what? Was he going to torture her, start to rape her over and over? What was he going to do to her?

Then it clicked. She thought about his books. What did they always have in common? What was it that made her gravitate towards them and why did she read them over and over?

He always had women as his main character. They were often pulled into these horrifying situations, but it was always a woman. Often, it was the woman who didn't live through the end of the book. They always ended up dying in some grueling and dramatic way that completed the arc and resolved the storyline... but the woman always died.

Especially in his early books, the ones before demons started to be an undercurrent to his writing. All his early books. It was always a woman struggling to survive, only to die horribly.

She tried to focus on just what he was saying. He was loosening one of her wrist straps.

"This book is getting stale. You need a chance to escape. Let's see what happens," Jacob said as he came close to freeing her wrist completely but stopped. She had room, and she might be able to free herself eventually. He stopped, though, and it wasn't enough that she could pull free and attack him. He knew that. She could see it in the smirk as he watched the realization come to her.

"Please don't do this."

Jacob turned from her and started to leave the room, but stopped. He just stood there, not looking back at her, but not really looking anywhere other than whatever lay beyond the room.

"I'll..." Lexi felt herself almost say she would do anything, and the mental image that flashed through her thoughts was her head nearing him as he unzipped his jeans. She tried to push the thought away and wasn't sure where it came from. She just needed him to keep from closing that door.

She was struggling with the restraint. Maybe if she could get him closer, she could get it free. Or maybe she should go to suck his penis. The thought of biting down and ripping it away from him, him screaming as he collapsed, writhing in pain, suddenly pushed away the tears.

He turned back to her, and she could see as he tried to get a read on her. Did he see her wheels turning and a new light in her eye at her plan? Did he see her as desperate and willing to do anything to be set free? Did he think she was the ditsy girl, or did he think she was a fighter? What did he see as he studied her intently?

He walked back to her, undoing his belt as he did. He moved so that he was close to her chair, and she could smell the strong odor of some smoke infused whisky cologne that she hadn't noticed before. He was undoing the zipper, working slowly as though he savored the moment.

Yeah, he's not going to be savoring it once I bite his cock off.

He reached in and she could smell the odor of sweat and semen already wafting out from the opening. If it smelled so bad like this, how was it going to be once he pulled it out? How bad was it going to taste?

Lexi had to struggle, fighting back the bile that was again threatening as it tickled the back of her throat. She grimaced as she forced herself to swallow it back down.

"Did you really think I brought you here just for sexual gratification? How shallow do you think I am?" he asked as he pulled his hand out and zipped his pants back up. He was fastening his belt when the anger rose inside of her, anger not bile this time, and it launched itself at him in the form of phlegm. She spit on him and saw that there were traces of bile as it coated the back of his hand.

He almost hit her in a brief moment when rage flashed through the room, and his face went red as he glared down at her. Then the emotion was gone, and the smirk returned. He wiped the spit from his hand, again using her shirt, and when he was finished, he re-tightened her restraint.

"It might be too soon for that after all," he said as he turned back to the door.

"You don't need me, psycho. You need your head examined." She tried to spit again, though he was already too far away.

"Oh, Lexi, I do need you. I need a new book, and you should make an excellent main character."

He left the room, closing and locking the door behind him.

MISSING PERSONS: LEXI PEABODY
VIDEO EXCERPT

Hey everyone! LexiSexyReads here again for another book recommendation. First off, though, I want to give everyone a huge thank you. Last week, I posted my very first video and introduced myself to BookFlix. Since then, you have all been so supportive and have been filling up my TBR with so many excellent recommendations.

This first one I just couldn't put down. Thank you, JSHorrorsby for turning me on to this new indie horror author as this guy is legit. This book was out there, and I have to tell you all about it.

So, the book is by this guy, Jacob Skulz. I'm not sure if that's his real name or what because Skulz seems a little too on the nose. Still, the guy's writing is fantastic. He really sells the gore and there is something about his characters that is really earnest. I'm guessing he based them on people he actually knew or something because he really nails it.

The book is called Dead Friends. It's about these two friends who are hiking and fall into a sinkhole and have no way to get out. Nearly the whole book is them in the sinkhole. There are some nightmares; there is them dealing with creatures, some creepy crawlies, some rodents, you name it. If you think it would live in a cave, it is probably in this book.

The time when the centipede or whatever it was crawled up Tina's nose! Ick! She squeezed it and felt all that goo running from her nostril down into her throat, making her gag.

BLA-ah. Gives me the shivers. Great job on the heebie jeebies, bub.

Then when Rose breaks her ankle, trying to climb out and is writhing in pain so that it slowly drives Tina insane...

I'm not going to give away the ending, but I'm just going to say there is cannibalism in this book, so if that is a trigger you may want to stay away.

From what I can find, this is Skulz's first novel and for a debut, I must say, I'm a fan. My own friend here, come here Ame!-

<video rustles and another voice is heard. >No, Lexi, I said no; I don't want to be in it. You do your thing.

<Video stills back to Lexi>

Well, I guess everyone's stuck with just me, but A here, she did tell me that if we ever get stuck in a hole; I get to eat her. Now all you boys out there, take that for what it's worth.

This is Skulz' first novel, and I gotta say; I give it 5 skulls, pun intended. I highly recommend and will be looking for more of Skulzy's books. Skulzy... I like it. So go check out some Skulzy. Check it out and make sure to hit the heart and follow. Until next time, creeps. Stay sexy.

CHAPTER 5

Amanda had called Lexi's mom first before calling the police, and she was glad she did. She didn't think she'd been able to handle any of it without her there. The woman was an unstoppable force that was not going to take shit from anyone.

Tanya, or Tee as she preferred being called by anyone who knew her, was a part of the Gen X generation and she was a hardcore bad ass. Every time Amanda met the woman, she always took control, didn't take lip from anyone and she always spoke her mind.

So, when the police finally did show up where Amanda and Tee waited by the abandoned car, the pair had already been there for a half hour and were not going to let the cops have an easy go of it. Amanda sensed that the two officers that arrived were quick to dismiss them, having dropped comments about Lexi "just out partying" and being a "college kid off doing their thing."

"She is not officially missing. How do you know she was taken?" the older officer said, who had a speckled gray beard and was wearing dark sunglasses. He was shorter than her but postured himself straight as though there was no intimidation from the taller woman. The shorter officer was younger, blond hair, but with the same stupid sunglasses. Amanda wanted to ask them if they bought them in bulk and got a discount, but she was too worried about her friend. Besides, Lexi was the sarcastic one between the two of them. Lexi would have been the one to say what Amanda was thinking. It was almost like her friend could read her mind.

"Okay, honey, now listen here. You see this car? You see how there is currently no driver in this car? Just how many twenty-year-olds do you know that leave their car to go for a stroll sometime in the middle of the night?" Tee was saying as she held her arms out like she was presenting the vehicle to them. Her agitation was clear in the sarcasm that coated each word as she spoke, her contempt for the officers gaslighting them obvious in every part of her being.

God, how Amanda admired her, wishing she could have that level of confidence.

"We don't know if it's been here all night." The shorter cop said, his voice gushing with that overly righteous confidence.

"Really. Hmm, if there was only a place nearby that probably has cameras and could review the footage. Some place that was maybe monitoring their parking lot." Tee turned from scowling at the police officers to looking over her shoulder at the entrance of the large department store. Not only were there plainly visible security cameras attached to the outside of the building, but could also be seen mounted to the lamps overhead as well. Amanda counted at least six cameras without really trying. She was sure there were more, but she felt Tee had clearly made the case.

"Ma'am, we can't just get footage from them without an active investigation, and there is no clear evidence to open one," the older cop said, already making his way back to their squad car.

"No clear evidence? What the hell do you call this?" Tee said.

"Well, we are standing in a store parking lot. Have you looked for her inside? She could be 'shopping'." The damn asshole of a younger cop air quoted as he opened his passenger door.

"Hey, we could just go inside and ask if they will allow us to see the footage. Are you guys willing to come in and at least humor us for that?" Amanda almost didn't recognize her own voice, surprised to hear herself speaking, but she realized she was going to have to be the voice of reason. As much as she appreciated and adored Tee, sometimes tact worked over sass, though the sass was so much more fun to watch.

The cops looked over the top of their squad car at each other, not saying anything, though Amanda could hear a voice coming over their radio. She was too far away from them to hear it, but she watched as the older cop reached for his radio.

"Yes, we're here now, going over the situation with the reporting party."

More of the radio voice that Amanda couldn't hear, but she watched the body language of the two officers squirm.

"The missing person is over eighteen and it has been less that twenty-four hours," the older cop said.

Amanda watched as the younger cop backed away from the open door and closed it. As the radio voice finished, the older officer was already walking in their direction.

"Let's check with the store. We'll see if they will let us watch the footage. Also, I'm told my captain is sending a detective to meet with you and will finish taking your statement."

"Why the change of heart, boys?" Tee was already leading the way towards the entrance.

"Captain heard from the dispatcher about the young woman meeting a guy in the middle of the night is now reported missing. She didn't want to lose any time waiting for the first twenty-four hours."

"She, huh?" Tee said and looked back to Amanda who was too shocked to really believe they were going to see the footage.

Though as they walked to the front of the store, her lunch went sour in her stomach. What was going to be on that video? If they did get to watch it, was she going to see her friend murdered? Kidnapped? Just what did happen last night?

Amanda wanted answers more than anything else, but was she going to be able to handle them? She wasn't so sure she could.

* * * *

"Play that back, show me again," the older officer said. He was leaning over the store manager's shoulder, and it was clear the manager was not comfortable with the intrusion into his personal space.

"There's nothing more to see. I've told you that. I've rewound it half a dozen times, and we checked each of the cameras. Playing it one more time is not going to change anything."

Amanda and Tee had already moved towards the back of the room. It was a tight fit for all four of them to be in a room the size of a large broom closet. Between the size and the heat from the store's computer servers, it kept the space ten degrees warmer than the outer hallway.

It wasn't the heat and the size that kept them back there...

For Amanda, it was the shock. She thought that's what it was, at least. She just couldn't believe it. She didn't want to believe it. Part of her wanted to hyperventilate and scream that it wasn't possible, that these things only happened to other people, not someone you knew. The other part of her wanted to collapse into a crying mess on the floor and just admit that her best friend was dead. With both emotions struggling to dominate her reasoning, she herself felt dead. That the war within her was too exhausting, so that there were no emotions to remain. It was all too much.

Tee, on the other hand, imploded.

When they first watched the video, the store manager found the footage from the front of the store and queued it to when Lexi's car pulled into the lot. The officer immediately looked at Tee and it was clear he was embarrassed by how he treated them earlier. The time stamp of the footage made it clear that Lexi wasn't just shopping.

Tee ignored him, keeping her eyes locked onto her daughter's car and watched as she sat there. Then they saw the lights of another car pulling into the lot. That was when the footage cut out for thirteen minutes and thirty-two seconds. That's how long the footage was missing, and when it came back, the car was empty and there was no sign of the other car that had been pulling in.

Tee lost it. Amanda watched as it happened.

"Where is she? Where is my little girl? Where is she?" Tee said, her voice cracking as she backed away from the monitors, her hand over her mouth as the first tears crusted the horizon of her eyes. She had been in a battle to keep them away, but by seeing what was and wasn't on the footage, she surrendered.

Amanda moved in close to her and wrapped her arm around her. Tee buried her face into Amanda's chest. Everybody paid little attention to them as the officer had the manager go through the footage of all the other cameras. The same thirteen minutes and thirty-two seconds were missing from all of them.

"How is that possible?" someone asked. She thought it was the older officer. The manager responded, though his voice was unsteady, not understanding his own explanation.

41

"The cameras are motion activated, so either it sensed there was no motion or there was some kind of jammer," the manager said.

"Not possible. Those things don't exist?" the officer said.

"They have cell jammers. The cameras work by being on the network. It would only take something interfering with the network to cut them off."

"Really?" The officer seemed surprised, though Amanda wasn't. She knew a little of what the manager was referring to, having taken a class at the junior college, but she was by far not an expert.

"Wait, that still doesn't make sense. The cameras have internal storage. They would still have recorded and uploaded the footage once the interference was gone. So no, I can't explain it."

"Run it again," the officer said.

After the third viewing, the officer turned to Tee, but then to Amanda, seeing how the older woman was struggling with what they were seeing.

"Do you know why she was here alone that time of night?"

"Because I refused to go with her. It's because of me that he took her. I should have been there, but she was being so dumb." Amanda started to ramble, fighting her own fresh wave of tears. It was hard to fight them. This was all her fault.

"Don't blame yourself, hun," Tee said, wiping away the mucus dripping from her nose as she met Amanda's eyes. "That girl has never had a sense of danger in her life. At first, I thought it was the ADHD, but lord help me, she would jump off a cliff without looking just because someone dared her. This was never your fault."

Amanda tried to accept it, as did the officer. Now, with his sunglasses removed, she could see his eyes, and she saw that he too was looking at her with a pained expression.

"It's nothing you did. Remember, she chose to come, even if you told her you weren't coming with her."

Amanda nodded but couldn't help as her eyes wandered back to the screen and the car that they could only see the headlights as it drove into the lot. She could just make out her friend sitting in the front seat of her car. Her head leaned against the car window, probably having drifted off as she waited.

Silence fell over the room, and the officer turned back to the monitors and asked the manager to play the footage again.

They played the footage over and over. Each time, the same thirteen minutes and thirty-two seconds were gone. By the last time, Tee was a crying mess in Amanda's arms and the girl felt her own stomach twist in fear with the realization that she may never see her best friend again.

CHAPTER 6

Lexi shivered; the temperature dropped to a point where she was having trouble not shaking uncontrollably. She wasn't sure if it was night or day. The temperature could have fallen overnight, but as far as she knew, he could have turned on some hidden AC and was trying to freeze her to death. In all his books, that's one thing she hadn't read about, someone freezing. Maybe that would be her.

Though how would he work in the demon? All his latest books had demons... or maybe he'd finally realized he'd run demons into the ground and was finally going back to his roots.

She didn't want to think about it. It was actually easy not thinking about what he had planned for her. She was too hungry to care. Her stomach had hurt earlier. She'd even been lightheaded for a while. Funny thing about hunger though, if you stay hungry long enough, the sensation goes away, and your stomach begins to feel like it's eating itself.

A headache was also pounding through her skull. She wasn't sure if it was from dehydration or the lack of caffeine. She was well below her daily intake and was known to be a real bitch if she didn't have her fix.

There was a click. She didn't look up as the door scraped across the ground, opening so he could enter.

"Good morning," he said in a cheerful voice, and she could smell coffee, the sweet aroma drifting into the room.

Somehow, even in her dehydrated state, she could feel the drool inside her mouth moistening her tongue. She looked up, hoping he would be carrying for her a plate of food and a morning cup of Joe.

He did have a coffee mug in his hand that was obviously just for him as he took a long sip. He watched her watching him. She could see his smirk behind the cup. The asshole was getting off on seeing how much she wanted his coffee. She could only imagine how it tasted, the bitter sweetness in that plain white coffee cup.

She struggled to take her eyes off of it but pulled them away to look at the man himself, taking in his appearance. His hair was a tangled mess, and his eyes were barely open, as though he had pulled himself out of bed only moments ago. His shirt was scrunched up, and he wore some sort of decorative Christmas pajama pants that were riddled with holes. The thin cloth of the pants screamed to be thrown away as they had long ago worn out, but the man stood there wearing them, failing to give in to common decency.

It was nowhere near Christmas time. What was behind those ugly ass pants? Did they mean something? They were old as fuck. Maybe even as old as his writing career.

Lexi thought back to his first couple of books. She had found out by making videos on him that while the book about the two hikers was his first released book, he had written a different book first. It was about a couple that had gone to a cabin in the woods and the wife was killed.

What was the title? She struggled to think through her hunger haze. She couldn't remember much about the book; she was too damn hungry. What the hell had happened?

Lexi realized that he was waiting for her to respond to him. She didn't. She kept watching him, waiting for any sense as to what this monster wanted.

He took another long drink from the mug, then looked at it.

"You know, I can't go a morning without my morning coffee. I've been watching some of your videos. It would appear that you're quite the connoisseur yourself. So many videos of you have a store-bought latte and reading one of my books. Aren't you excited? You finally get to be a character in one."

Lexi continued to glare at him. Her stomach rolling, growling loudly in the small room. Her hunger had reached the point where she ground her teeth together and clenched her fists, just wanting to get free from the restraints and attack him. Everything he said was like nails on a chalkboard and drove her to wanting to tear his face to shreds of flesh so that she could peel them away.

"You know, for a long time, I never had a lot of positive memories of my dad. I carried a lot of resentment towards him, you know, thinking of the mental and physical abuse. Though over time, I started to remember little things.

"He was an alcoholic who, if given the choice, would have been passed out in a bar every night. Instead, he was home while my mom worked second shift. He may not have been there to talk or to treat me well, but he was there. There's something to be said for that."

Jacob looked past her as though he was getting lost in a memory. He then smiled and smelled the cup of coffee in his hands.

"There's a lot to be said about smells. I remember how many nights while he would be there, he would cook popcorn on the stove. He wasn't one of these microwave popcorn types. No, he was a truest. Put some oil in a pot, some popcorn kernels and there you go, filling the house with that heavenly fragrance."

Lexi grounded her teeth until her jaw hurt. She could feel wetness in her eyes, but the tears did not come. She could smell the coffee and just wanted it. Right then, there was nothing more in this world that she wanted.

She started to pull at her restraints, viciously fighting against them, struggling to get any give, anything to break free on merit strength alone.

"The other scent I associate with him is coffee. It's probably rooted in my own addiction to this blessed brew.

"I remember every morning waking up an hour before my own alarm and I would hear him in the kitchen. He would be tooling around, getting a cup ready as the initial pot brewed. On mornings I would need to piss, I would go and find him taking a shit with the door wide open and was thankful that scent didn't spread through our house like the coffee did. I'd have to go outside and take my piss off the back porch.

"But the smell of coffee. It was every morning and was such a blessed aroma to wake up to. He drank his black, pure and bitter. Maybe it is my love for him and those memories that kindled my addiction. Definitely not the taste as my own cup is corrupted with so much sugar and creamer that there is little remnant of its original flavor."

Jacob finished the coffee in a long final gulp, then turned over the cup so the final few drops fell to the floor to signal his point that he was done. None of it offered to her.

"I'm thinking I'll have some bacon and eggs. Seems like a good morning for it. I'll check back on you later."

The door slammed shut, and Lexi unleashed, frantically pulling at her restraints even harder than before, putting everything she had to break free with a strength she was unaware she'd had. Her anger fueled by rage and hunger had her wanting to rip into that asshole and tear him apart. To fight, to scream, to rip his still beating heart out.

Lexi wasn't sure, but she thought, as she fought against the bonds, that she could feel them getting looser. She struggled even harder against them.

48

* * * *

She wasn't sure how long it had been. She continued to fight against her restraints for as long as she could before her anger lost steam and her strength waned. Her stomach was still growling and writhing inside her to the point that she couldn't think straight, and all she could focus on was food and coffee. Any form of sustenance would be worth selling her soul.

Her tears returned, though they were barely more than a wetness to her eyes as the thick crust around them was hard to breach.

It was hard to find the strength to raise her head. It was exhausting to do anything.

The door clicked, and she heard that scraping sound as it was pushed open.

Then the smell of eggs and bacon assaulted her, and she forced herself to look up. Jacob was carrying in a tray of food and coffee. He lowered it to the floor, using the space he had previously cleared amongst the bones to set it down. She could see it all there on a plate, nicely laid out for her to eat. There actually were scrambled eggs, bacon, even toast and a steaming hot cup of black coffee.

It looked like desire on a plate, and she had never wanted to have something so much in her life. Even with her dehydrated self, she could feel the saliva filling her mouth to the point that drool escaped from the corner.

He stood and stepped away from her, watching her with a knowing smile. She glared at him, biting as much of her anger as her exhaustion allowed.

"I thought you might be getting hungry," he said.

It smelled so good. Her stomach was screaming for it but twisting at the same time in disgust. She was starving, but she was hungry to the point where food was desirable and revolting at the same time. She wanted it, but also didn't think she could eat all of it.

It occurred to her, if she was to eat, he would have to undo her restraints unless he planned to feed it to her. This was going to be her chance. She was going to have to rush him as soon as her hands were free; she had to grab him. He was larger, and she was weak from already being down there too long, but it was her only chance. She had to try.

His smile slipped into a smirk as though he were reading her mind.

Had he been? Is that why he stood there? Was he waiting for her to figure that out?

Of course he was. That's what he was waiting on. That makes for a more interesting story. You have to have action and thrills. He was waiting for her to attack him. That's what he needed for his next book.

It didn't matter, though. She needed to try. No matter if he was expecting it and was prepared for it. She couldn't just give up and die.

Though if you die, you kill his story too. Then neither of you win...

No, she wasn't going to give in that way. Not in a million years.

"Bon appetite," he finally said and closed the door. She hadn't noticed he moved toward it and had just left her there.

The coffee, that intoxicating aroma plagued her senses as it mixed with the bacon and the eggs. She looked at the tray longingly, wanting so much to devour it all. She noticed that he left her with no utensils, so she would have to use her hands, but she would do that. She could see herself stuffing handfuls into her mouth, the yellow globs of it rubbed along her cheeks as she tried to force as much as she could down her throat.

She wanted the food. She just had to find a way to get to it.

She looked at the ropes around her right hand and shifted it, revealing the frayed cord that held her in place. Where it rubbed along the metal of her chair, she saw how more and more strands were being stripped away.

MISSING PERSONS: LEXI PEABODY
VIDEO EXCERPT

Hey Flix fam! LexiSexyReads here again for another book recommendation, and guess what? I have the latest Skulzy! I just got it from Bound books in town because remember everyone, shop local and shop indie. Always make sure to support your independent bookstores.

Okay, now the book, and this one was a special order because this is his first book. That's right, I got it. Madness, the book about a young writer and his wife as they travel to a new cabin in the woods that he just bought. They are trying out the new place; the wife gets hurt and then instead of getting help; he watches as she slowly dies.

Now, that's just the first part of this book. This sicko then goes back to his life, sells a story that is eerily like what he just did, becomes all famous, gets a girlfriend and takes her out to the cabin. There, she finds the petrified corpse of his ex-wife on the bed where he lets her die. He then devolves as he starts referring to his girlfriend by his ex's name and starts chasing her.

I'm not going to give away the end, but I'll tell you it does not end how one would think. This is an intense book that hits all the notes. He really understands his characters, and he makes them all so distinct that you would not mistake the girlfriend for the wife.

I think you guys know where I'm going with this. 5 skulls, definite read, I highly recommend. Now, stay sexy everyone, Sexy Lexi here saying, I'm out.

CHAPTER 7

Amanda wasn't sure what she should be doing. She had woken up that morning and the first thing she had done was check her phone for any new messages. It was the same thing she had done throughout the night, waking up as she jumped from one terrifying nightmare to another, only taking short breaks in between to see if there was any news.

So far, her phone had stayed notification free. There was nothing.

Should she call the police and check in? No, the police wouldn't be reaching out to her anyway, they would be reaching out to Tee. If she reached out to anyone, it should be her.

Amanda grabbed her phone, debating as she looked up Tee's number in her contacts. She paused with her phone in her hand, unsure if she should? She didn't consciously do it, but she tapped the number, and the phone started chirping.

It rang for a while to the point that Amanda was surprised it hadn't already switched over to voicemail and Amanda could feel her heart rising in her chest. It hurt to breathe, and she felt that familiar wetness at the corner of her eyes. No tears were coming, but she felt on edge, ready to burst.

"Hello," a very tired older man's voice came from the other side of the call. It wasn't Tee, and she didn't recognize it.

"Hello, I was calling for Tee. Is she available?"

"Who?"

"Tee? Lexi's mom? I'm Amanda, Lexi's best friend."

"Lexi? Do you know where she is?"

"I don't. That's why I was calling. Can I speak to Tee please?" Amanda did not like how frantic the guy had suddenly become. Why couldn't he just get the phone over to Tee? What was going on?

"She's not available right now."

"But isn't this her cell phone?"

Amanda started to feel that knot in her chest expand. She didn't know who the hell this guy was, but was starting to imagine it being the guy who had Lexi. Jacob Skulz was an older guy, right? And it made sense. Get the daughter, then go after the mother, especially if she's looking for her.

Amanda thought about immediately hanging up the phone and calling 9-1-1.

"Yeah, it's her phone. Listen. She's not well. It might be best to not call her for a while," the voice said.

"Who is this? What do you mean, she's not well?" The panic was rising into Amanda's voice, and she couldn't help it. Just who the hell was this guy? She should call the police. She was sure of it now. "What about her daughter?"

"Listen. Let the police search for her. If she really is missing, they'll find her, but Tee, she's not handling it well. Jack has sent her away for some rest. Jack'll take care of it."

"Who are you? Can I speak to Jack then?"

"Jack, there's a girl here trying to get ahold of your wife. You up to talking to her?"

There was silence on the other end of the call, then another tired voice spoke.

"Hello?" Amanda assumed this was Jack. Amanda tried to remember if she'd ever met the man. He wasn't home much, always on the road for work, so he was never around, and Lexi didn't talk about him. Amanda didn't think they were close. She did remember that Jack was Lexi's stepfather, and that caused issues, so Lexi didn't live at home anymore.

"Hello, Mr. Peabody?"

"Yes."

She could hear the frustration growing in his voice.

"Is Tee okay?"

"Not really. She's had another episode and is in the hospital. Look, is Lexi with you? Tanya was not making any sense before I had to take her. Sounded like she went off her meds and I figured Lexi might be hiding at your place."

"No, Lexi's missing. Someone took her. Tee and I filed a report yesterday."

"Look, Tanya is sick. She's not in her right mind. It happens when she stops taking her medication."

"Mr. Peabody, I'm the one who reported her missing. It's not Tee. Your daughter was taken. We saw the video."

"You've seen video? You saw my stepdaughter get kidnapped?"

"Well, no. The video cut out, but the cops were convinced, and she was going to meet some strange man."

"Yeah?"

"Yeah."

"Look, I love my wife, and I love my stepdaughter, but they both have their share of problems. You've been Lexi's friend for what, a couple years now? I know it was after this new job and I went over the road, so we've never gotten to know one another, so I don't know the type of person you are. You might be just as crazy as those two.

"But that being said, it's just as likely that Lexi ran off with the guy. You can't go assuming that everyone's out to get you. They're not."

"But-"

"Look, I get that your heart is in the right place. I'm going to text you my number, so you have it. If the police do find anything or I hear any different, I'll let you know, and I hope you would do the same.

"Until then, try not to stress yourself. Let the police do their thing. I'm just saying, I bet this all turns out to be a big load of nothin'."

Amanda let the call run its course with their farewells and tossed her phone onto the bed after it disconnected. She was frustrated. How could he not worry about his missing daughter? She wanted to call him back and fight with him, but what would she say? He seemed so sure of himself that they were all crazy. Lexi would not run off with some stranger...

Though he was her favorite author. She adored his books. She was always frustrated when she missed any of his book signings or convention appearances because they lived too far away. Skulz was known for being very private. He didn't do many of them, so when he did, it was always a big deal for her.

As Amanda sat in her desk chair and thought about it, she could start making a case that maybe her friend did run off, but wouldn't she call her, send her a message letting her know Lexi was okay?

Amanda grabbed her tablet and opened their favorite streaming app, immediately searching to find Lexi's profile. Lexi never went for more than twelve hours without cutting a video, so even if she had run off, she would have made something to release. Lexi was still thinking she could become Flix famous and posted videos to the service as often as she could, always trying to go viral.

Nothing. Just her latest video was there, the one where she mentioned she was finally going to be able to meet her favorite author. Lexi was smiling so brightly in that video, her eyes danced with joy.

The video only had a hundred views. Less than her average. It was because she had been in a hurry to post it and hadn't added any hashtags.

Amanda watched the video again, wishing that by giving the video more views, maybe it would somehow get her friend to call her, tell her she was okay. The phone never rang. She kept watching the video, over and over, trying to force it to somehow work, to somehow find her friend.

On about the twelfth try, she watched the faces and names of other people who liked the video. She watched, and she recognized his name as it scrolled by. He hearted her video. She clicked on it, and there he was, his posed face looking back at her. He had his face tilted forward like he was trying to do a creepy, moody expression as he looked at the camera.

That was the man. This was the person who had taken her best friend.

CHAPTER 8

The door unlocked, the loud clinking sound of its release sending a shockwave through her. She felt it in her bones as it jolted her from how she'd allowed herself to daze out.

Just how long had she been down there?

She opened her eyes and saw that the plate of food was still on the floor where he'd left it. The eggs looked like a congealed blob while the coffee was black oil in a cup. Only the bacon still looked moderately edible, but wasn't that part of the magic that was bacon?

Her mouth tried to produce saliva looking at the wondrous strip of pig fat, but that only intensified the cottonmouth, making her mouth a dry mesh that felt true to the name. She wouldn't be surprised if she started producing cotton from her own mouth with how it felt.

The rambling thoughts were beginning to make less sense. It was getting hard to control them. The hunger, exhaustion, dehydration, all of them made it near impossible to think straight.

The door slowly scraped open, and he emerged. He was dressed in a semblance of normal clothes. Though nothing you would see being worn to a place of business. He wore regular-looking blue jeans and a black shirt with some geeky slogan she thought was some reference to an 80s movie. If she could get through this damn brain fog, she was sure she knew it, but for now, it was just out of reach.

"Hmm," was all he said as he looked at the plate and then back at her. He seemed to be disapproving that the plate was untouched, but what the hell? She was still restrained to this damn chair. Did he expect her to break free and ravage the food?

She kept watching him, waiting.

"This isn't working," he finally said as he scanned the room, stopping to look at something behind her, something she couldn't see.

"You know, when you replied to my message, gave me a place to meet, I really thought you had MC potential. That you could carry a story all by yourself."

Jacob started walking around behind her, clearing a path through the bones as he walked. Her heart beat faster when she couldn't see him, suddenly not sure what he was going to do. She hadn't been watching his hands; did he have a razor or something small tucked behind his back as he walked? Had his hand purposely been turned away so she couldn't see? She tried to remember, but any thinking was becoming so difficult when all she could focus on was the pain in her stomach.

Oh no, he was going to do it. He was going to end the story.

She tried to see him, turning to find where he was, listening to see if she could hear him breathing.

Then she felt his breath on her neck and knew he was right behind her, almost touching her. She could smell the stench of stale coffee as he spoke.

"You are my biggest disappointment." He let out a long breath that drifted off to a sigh as he stood and walked back around to face her. "I really thought you could carry this story by yourself."

He didn't have a knife in his hands. She watched them as he spoke and saw how he opened them wide. She remembered that in watching videos of him. He liked to

62

talk with his hands, always moving them to express himself when he gave readings and presentations.

She almost felt herself sighing a mental breath of relief until she noticed the bulge in his pocket. The one he kept patting to make sure it was there. She was sure it was a subconscious tick with him as he did it every so often, a subtle pat as he continued on.

She had been watching his hands as he droned on but looked at him when she realized he had stopped talking and was studying her.

"I mean, you've noticed it? All my books, two characters playing off one another. It's become my own trope. The review of my last book, it's all getting so repetitive. I'm a one-trick pony, always having a predator and a prey.

"So just once, I wanted to have one main character. Someone who could carry a story all the way through, and I thought you were the one. I watched your videos and thought, hey, this is a person who had a rough life. I bet she could carry a story, be a fighter, really struggle and be a survivor.

"I had some really high hopes for you."

Lexi's breath caught as he moved to pull out the rectangular object from his pants. She wished she was relieved when he pulled out his phone instead of a knife.

"I've been keeping tabs on your friends. Your friend Amanda, she started following me. She even sent me a message. Here, you want to see it?"

He leaned forward, showing his screen to her, and she saw the familiar inbox of the Flix app. She saw Amanda's profile picture just above a conversation the two of them had been having. She didn't get a chance to read all of it before he pulled the phone away.

"She heard you were getting a signed advanced copy and wanted to know if she could get one. She gave me her address and everything. Does she really think I'm that dumb to just show up? Well, I won't be going there, but I've got friends.

"I think it's time we started slicing this story up. Don't you?"

Lexi leapt forward with all her strength, putting as much weight as she could into breaking her bonds. They held, but she could feel them loosening.

Jacob hadn't taken any chances that she was going to get him as he had quickly dashed to the door and hid behind it, partly pulling it closed. He stopped when he realized she wasn't getting free and smiled as he watched her struggle. She saw how he enjoyed watching her, the longing apparent in how he looked at her. He started laughing, and that fueled her to try harder. She felt like she almost had her right arm loosened to a point where she could pull her hand free.

"There we go tiger. Come get some. I knew there was a fighter in there," he said, almost dancing. "You know, if you keep that up, I might not have to get your friend after all."

"What-" Lexi tried to speak, but it was hard to push the words through her chapped lips and rough throat. "Do you... want... from me?"

"Oh, hun, you still haven't figured that out? I want you to be my main character."

When her fighting against the restraints calmed, he eased back into the room and grabbed the tray of food.

"Probably a good thing you didn't get to the food. I had it laced with a strong dose of LSD. Too bad, as I'm certain it would have been a hell of a trip."

He took the tray and started to close the door before looking back at her one last time.

"So, has Max visited you yet? If not, I'm sure he will. He always loves to play with the new guests. I don't always put him in the books, but he's always here."

The door closed, and she heard the lock click back into place.

"You don't need to worry about him. I'm right here. I'm always here," a gravelly voice whispered softly into her ear, though she didn't feel its breath. On her other shoulder, she could feel something sharp coming down one by one, like four fingers slowly drumming along the flesh. "I'm the one you need to worry about, and I'm always here. Do you want to play with me?"

Then the light went out in the room, and Lexi screamed.

MISSING PERSONS: LEXI PEABODY
VIDEO EXCERPT

Hey Flix fam, LexiSexyReads here again. Just a quick one for you tonight as I'm tired, but I stayed up late this time because I could not put this one down. It's another Skulz novel, and this one was not well received. I've seen a lot of negative reviews out there saying that Skulz has lost his touch and that he's just rehashing his older work.

Well, to all the haters out there, you can just keep hating because I liked the book. The ending was a little weak. It felt like it just needed something more, but the rest of the book was downright creepy.

So, the book returns to small town Wisconsin and this time an ancient evil has been awakened and comes in the form of darkness. Anytime. Anywhere there is a shadow, this entity could be coming out of the dark to grab you and pull you into its own hidden depths.

For the most part, the entity loves going after the children and has all the parents up in arms, worried about who is going to be next.

What truly makes this book creepy is that it takes the everyday fear of the dark and turns it against you. I loved that. Any shadow or darkness, it could come out of anywhere and pull you into its depths. The night literally comes alive and takes you into that void. It plays into your fear of the dark.

I mean, just imagine walking down a dark street at night, and you notice that it is getting darker. Like, you watch as the streetlight above you just disappears. Then you notice that you can't see anything around you. It's all pitch black. You try to scream, but it is stolen from you. The dark gets closer, until finally all is lost, and it has you.

This book really had me turning on every light and had me worried about all those shadows in the corner. I highly recommend it. It's called Into Darkness and is another of his harder to find books, but if you can get a copy, you won't regret it.

LexiSexy telling you to check it out. And now I'm getting some sleep... though I'll be sleeping with the lights on tonight.

CHAPTER 9

Amanda heard the pounding on the door and rolled over on her bed to look at the clock, not sure what time it was. The sun shining through her window told her it was already later than she had planned, and she'd slept through her alarm.

What did it matter? It wasn't like she was planning on going to school or work today. She'd blown off both for the last few days now, as she couldn't concentrate on any of it. School, she doubted anyone even noticed, but work, she had already been told one more missed shift without a good excuse, and she was done.

Maybe she would go in tonight. She still wasn't sure.

The doorbell rang again, and there was more pounding on the door.

What if it was him? This could be her chance to... to do what? She hadn't thought that far into her plan yet, but it was finally enough motivation that she pulled herself out of bed and grabbed a pair of jeans from the floor.

"Hold on," she called out as she pulled on the pants. She grabbed her phone and crossed the obstacle course that was her studio apartment, junk scattered all over the place as she made her way to the door.

As she neared it, she pulled out the taser she had charging. It was plugged into the outlet in her bathroom, and she wanted to be ready.

Why had she given him her address? That was so dumb. She'd been drinking. She was tired, stressed, worried about her friend. Damn, why did she do that?

She looked through the peephole and saw a shorter, angry looking woman wearing a suit pacing back and forth in front of her door.

It's not him...

She sighed in relief as she pulled the door open. The woman standing there looked annoyed, but then saw the Taser still in Amanda's hand.

"Ms. Fields?" the woman said.

"Yes?" Amanda scanned the hallway but didn't see anyone else.

"You filed a missing person report on Alexa Peabody, correct?"

"Excuse me, who are you?"

"Detective Crews. I'm here to follow up. Do you mind if I come in?"

"We could, but the café downstairs would be more comfortable." Amanda looked over her shoulder and the state of her place. "And cleaner."

The detective followed her gaze and nodded.

"We can do that."

"Okay. Give me a minute and I'll meet you down there?"

"Sure."

Amanda nodded and closed the door.

A few minutes later, she was walking into the little café that was built into the outside corner of her apartment complex. She wished she could have just gone from the lobby of her building into the coffee shop, but unfortunately, she still had to go outside, walk to the corner and come in from the outside. It was a real pain on rainy days and during the winter.

Still, the coffee was great, so she lived with the minor inconvenience.

Amanda saw the detective sitting at a table in the back, and found herself unsure of how she should proceed. What was the proper etiquette? Should she order her coffee and then go over, or was it bad to leave the detective waiting? She decided to walk over to the detective first.

"Do you mind if I order first?" Amanda said, as she walked up to the table.

"Go right ahead."

"Thank you." Amanda wasn't sure why she was thanking the woman. It wasn't like she needed the woman's permission. She decided not to let it weigh on her and ordered her normal caramel iced latte. Lexi always went for hot drinks, even at the peak of summer, but Amanda preferred the cold.

With her drink in hand, she returned to the table, wishing she had gone with a warm drink after all. She noticed her hands shaking at the counter and now wished she had a warm cup to hold to try to hide it from the detective.

"I take it you haven't heard from your friend?" the detective said as Amanda sat down.

She shook her head as she took that first drink and felt the sensation of the cool liquid as it flowed into her, through her, already starting to fire her into wakefulness.

"I think I did something stupid. I gave the guy who took her my address." Amanda blurted out as soon as she finished taking that first drink. Damn, she was not awake enough for this and should not have just blurted that out.

"Wait, what? What do you mean you gave-" the detective was visibly shaken and reeled from how Amanda just broke the ice. "How did you find him? What were you thinking? That's one of the dumbest things I think I've ever seen anyone do."

Amanda kept her head low, focusing on her ice latte. With the vitriol being spewed at her, it no longer tasted sweet and invigorating.

"I know. I just- I need to find her. It's my fault. I should have been there. I should have gone with."

"I just don't get you young people. You know, in my day, we were taught things like stranger danger. You knew not to get into a creeps van, or meet some weirdo in a parking lot in the middle of the night. Or give the same creep your address."

Detective Crews took a long calming breath, closing her eyes and putting her hands on the table before letting it out slowly.

"Let's start over. I am looking into your friend's disappearance. First question, she's still missing, I assume. I mean, you wouldn't message this guy if she wasn't."

Amanda, keeping her eyes locked on her drink, nodded.

"Okay. I can't get in yet to see her mother and the stepdad is being a tool, so I'm going to need you to give me as much information as you can.

"Let's start with showing me this guy's online profile and the messages you sent him. In your initial report, you put in there that he is an independent author whose pen name is Jacob Skulz, one 'L'."

Amanda unlocked her phone and opened the Flix app. Within a few clicks, she found his profile, the profile picture of an older, silver-haired man smiling, looking at her over a mug of Guinness in some pub. His smile was more of a smirk as one corner of his lips tilted in a knowing, mocking way she hadn't noticed before. It was like, 'Hey, little girl, I've got a secret. I have your friend locked away somewhere and you'll never be able to find her.'

She handed the phone to the officer, who glanced at it before looking up at her, confused.

"What's going on here?"

"What do you mean?" the detective was handing her back the phone.

"Why's the profile blurry?"

Amanda looked at her phone. She didn't see anything that was blurry. She saw that smirking face, the bio, the profile that said he lived in River Falls, Wisconsin. It was all there.

"I don't see anything wrong," Amanda said, handing back the phone, but before the detective could take it from her, she grabbed Amanda's hand and held it while looking at the screen.

"You don't see that as blurry?"

"No, why?"

Detective Crews took out her own phone.

"What's the app called?"

"Flix."

"And it's a public profile?"

"Yeah, it's his author account."

Amanda watched as the detective downloaded the app and created an account.

"And it was J-A-C-O-B S-K-U-L-Z."

Amanda nodded 'Yes' while struggling with her own impulse to grab her phone and start doing her own scrolling. She hadn't had a chance yet to check her feed. She wasn't even sure why, but just wanted to scroll through while she was waiting on the detective.

The detective made a face.

"Not finding him?"

"Well, I see one Jacob Skulz come up in the search, but it's doing the same thing. It's blurred even when I open the profile."

The detective held up the phone to Amanda, but she didn't get it. She could see the profile just fine.

"What do you mean? It's clear to me," Amanda said as she sat back in her seat.

"What?" the detective looked back at her phone. "You don't see that blur?"

"I don't see any blur."

"What the hell?" the detective started searching through her phone and then back to typing on the keypad. "It keeps doing it. Okay, I'll have someone look into that. Now you said you gave your address. Why, what happened?"

"I-" Amanda started but then lost her words again. At least this time, she knew she wasn't going to blurt out something stupid, but she also had no idea where to start. "I'm not- I hadn't been taking this too well. I don't have many friends. I mean, look at me."

Amanda waved her hands down as though she was presenting herself to some audience.

"I'm not much to look at. When Lexi and I had class together, we got paired up in some exercise. We talked and got along. Lexi and I didn't have a good home life. Books were our escape, and we loved to talk about them. She leaned into horror. I loved romance, and we found a common middle ground in dark romance.

"She lived in Bloomington. I lived in Morton at the time and realized we both loved hanging out in Bobzbay Books and Coffee Hound. Somehow, we always missed one another or just never noticed each other. I tend not to pay attention a lot to what's going on around me."

It was obvious the detective was getting annoyed. She tried to hide it well. She wasn't checking her watch or phone or anything, but her face tightened, and jaw clenched. Amanda thought she was just waiting for her to quit talking long enough to ask her to move the story along.

"I'm sorry. Okay, but so, Lexi and I hang out a lot. We're there for each other. When she decided she wanted to become an influencer, I supported her. She got caught up in making bookflix videos, reviewing books. It's a thing and authors even, like, send you free books to get highlighted and reviewed. She was trying to get popular at it.

"But Lexi was also getting addicted to it. I make a video occasionally, and they get a couple of likes, but Lexi felt she needed to make multiple videos a day, do livestreams, all of it. She was trying to become Flix famous.

"I- know I got off topic, but you see, Lexi and I, she's really all I got. I don't have many friends. I have my books. I love my books. I love talking about books. Lexi understood that.

"So, when she went missing, I just don't know how to be alone anymore. I had some wine and then had some more. Before I knew it, the bottle was gone, and I'd opened another one. I hadn't been to work or school, nor did I care to go. I drank, and just- I just wanted my friend. I wanted to be with her."

"So, what, you trying to do suicide by serial killer? If he is, I'm just sayin' that's what it sounds like you just said." Detective Crews glared at her, and Amanda shifted in her seat. The glare softened as something shifted in the older woman. Amanda could see that the detective was upset, but her jaw had also unclenched, and her eyes turned kind with a hint of sadness as she studied her.

"I was drunk."

"People do stupid things when they drink."

"I normally don't. Drink that much, I mean. I do stupid things all the time. Locked my keys in my car the other day. That was fun."

"Okay. So, you're forgetful and currently self-destructive. Do you have anyone that you can talk to?"

"What do you mean? I told you; I don't really have any other friends."

"No, I mean a therapist. Someone that can help keep you from messaging possible kidnappers."

"No, I can't afford anything like that. It's okay though, I'm fine."

"Really? Because you don't sound like it."

"Can we just quit talking about me and start talking about what you're going to do to find my best friend?"

"Okay, so the original investigation hadn't been able to find anything on this Jacob Skulz. They couldn't find his profile, his website, and couldn't even find any books by him. I took over the case and see now why they couldn't, though I can't explain it.

"You say his profile shows that he is from River Falls, Wisconsin. That puts it over state lines, so as soon as we are done talking, I am going to call in the Feds. Had I known sooner about Wisconsin, we'd have called them already. This puts them at a disadvantage."

"Hey, I told you about the author. Why can't you find him? Why can't you just look him up in some database and go get the guy, save my friend if she's still alive?"

"That is something I'm going to be bringing up. I'm going to get them here and have them look into why his profile keeps blurring. Until then-" Detective Crews looked Amanda straight in the eye, locking her gaze. This woman seemed truly concerned for her. "You just put yourself on his radar. You are not safe. Do not do anything stupid. Don't go anywhere by yourself, don't walk to your car alone, don't leave your apartment by yourself. Call family, stay at your parents, whatever you need to do, just don't do it alone."

Amanda looked at her drink. She hadn't realized she was nearly done with it. It was down to the last remnants, and she'd casually zoned out as she swirled the mixture into the whipped cream while she played with her straw.

Had the detective not heard anything? Amanda was sure she had just told this woman that there was no one else. She had Lexi. That was who she went to. Her parents were useless and had always been unavailable. Amanda had been so thankful for her eighteenth birthday and moving away. They lived nearly forty minutes north from there in a town with just under a thousand people. There wasn't even a police department, no one to call in an emergency that would get there in a timely manner.

Plus, going home would mean having to face them, and after two years, she still wasn't ready. No, her parents weren't an option.

"You don't have anyone you could stay with?"

Amanda shook her head.

"Stay in your apartment. Once the feds get here, I'll get them to you as quickly as possible. Until then, stay put and lock your doors. Don't open them for anything."

Amanda nodded.

"Okay. Let me walk you back to your place."

CHAPTER 10

Lexi felt something cold slithering around her leg. It was smooth and solid, like firm muscle, as it pressed against her. She felt the throbbing as it rippled, pulsing as whatever it was used its body to move. It wrapped around her calves and then was on top of her thighs. Something fluttered from where she assumed was its head... and she knew it had to be a snake. It's forked tongue touching her, getting a sense of her.

Snakes? Why did it have to be snakes? She hated snakes. Her body tensed up, and she wanted to flap her thighs together and shake the thing off her, but she felt it tighten, compressing her lower leg, making sure it had a firm grip on her. It was like it was reading her mind and knew she wanted to get rid of it.

"I wouldn't do that if I was you," the guttural voice said, seductive as it whispered softly into her ear. Her stomach twisted, disgusted in response.

It moved higher up her thigh. She still couldn't tell how long it was, as it was still thick and meaty all the way down to her foot, with no hint of being close to its tail.

"Please-" Lexi sobbed, her gravelly voice barely above a whisper as it was hard to form words. "Get it away from me."

"Will you let me in?"

"Who are you? What do you want from me?"

"Oh, Lexi, I want to be in you. In all of you and feel your skin around me, hugging like warm, fresh baked bread. Have you ever stuck your penis in a loaf freshly cooled from the oven? Oh, you don't have a penis.

"I want to be your bread penis. I want to be warm and inside you, filling you, making you more than what you are. Will you let me in?"

She could feel the snake getting closer to her womanly bits and clenched up, tightening her thighs together. The snake lowered itself so it was pushing between them, and she could feel the continuing flick of that tongue as it moved.

"Let me in."

"No!" Lexi screamed, finding a reservoir of anger rising up in her. She felt the air shift in the room, all the heat being sucked out and that soul freezing chill that surrounded her that morning came rushing back.

The snake was gone. She felt the presence behind her back away.

"I'll be back for you. Until later."

The single light in the room shifted back into existence. It wasn't like it was suddenly turned back on, but instead whatever had kept its light from shining faded away.

MISSING PERSONS: LEXI PEABODY
VIDEO EXCERPT

Hey Flix fam, LexiSexy here with another book review, and you guessed it, it is another Jacob Skulz novel.

Okay, so this one, this one is just...wow. I mean, this is just a crazy read. It was fun, but kinda scary, and just a strange tongue-in-cheek book that was a little different from your normal Skulzy.

What's the name? Well, let me tell you about this one first.

First let me set the stage...

(Lexi looks at something offscreen and then an eerily slowed down, creepy version of Itsy Bitsy spider starts playing.)

So, imagine if you will, the craziest ex you've ever had. Now, imagine that after breaking up, they go out of their way to attempt to learn witchcraft so that they can curse you.

Now, we have a woman who is already not all there, and she is trying to find any book that she can on witchcraft. She finds books on Wicca, witchcraft, voodoo, satanism, but she's not trying to understand any of them or get their core beliefs. She just wants to curse her ex.

So, what happens when you play with magic that you don't understand? You end up conjuring creepy crawlers from another plane of existence that wreak their little havoc on you. That's what.

She tries to get her ex-boyfriend to help, only to have a monster escape from her and eat him.

It only gets crazier from there.

So, what's the book? 'Death Cooch' by Jacob Skulz. Check it out.

Sexy Lexi here, telling everyone to stay sexy.

CHAPTER 11

The light had barely returned and Lexi found herself fighting against the restraints, slamming everything she had into it. Her arm had been loose before; she was close; she felt like she was on the verge of getting it free. It wasn't going to take much more.

There it was. She felt it slip, her hand suddenly free. Her wrist was bleeding and covered in dirt. Much of that had dripped down onto her hand as she pulled through the restraint and now her fingers were wet and slippery. It made it difficult as she reached across to fight with the clasp still holding her left wrist. Her fingers didn't want to cooperate, shaking with exhaustion as she fumbled with the simple mechanism.

"Come on," she rasped, quickly growing frustrated as her freed hand didn't want to work properly. Why couldn't she just undo the thing? She almost had it; she had one hand free. She should be able to do this. It was a simple buckle, something that she'd dealt with regularly, so why couldn't she get the damn thing to open?

"Come on, little rabbit, you're so close," the other voice said. She'd thought the thing had left the room. She couldn't feel its presence anymore. Had she even heard it? She wasn't sure she trusted her ears anymore in the unbearable silence of the room.

She finally was able to pull up the metal pin of the clasp and worked to pull back the leather so it could slip through the hole. If she could get it, then the strip of leather would slide through the rest of the metal and her hand would be loose. She was wriggling to get it free, but it slipped, and the metal pin slid under her nail. She felt the sharp tinge of pain as it stabbed into the sensitive flesh below and now more blood was dripping.

"Fuck!" she cursed at it, pulling her hand away, not paying attention as she brought it to her mouth to suck at it. The blood was wet against her dry lips, and it moistened them as she sucked it from her freshly bleeding finger. The copper taste was sour as it danced along her tongue, but she found herself licking at it. It was wet, it was somehow nourishing, and she found it awakening something deep within her mind. It was pushing away some of the fog that had taken root in her thoughts.

As the blood from her finger slowed, she started licking the rest of the blood from her hand. It was somewhat dried already, but she was trying to get as much of it as possible. She devoured as much as she could until her hand was no longer dripping. Both her wrist and finger had stopped bleeding but were stained red.

She went back to working on the clasp, grimacing as her thumb ached with the stabbing pain. She was careful not to put too much pressure on and it was easier to work with the clasp now that her hand wasn't a wet mess of her own fluids.

Her fingers fumbled but found purchase seconds later, and the leather strap was free. Her hand was finally able to be pulled back, loose from the restraint, but doing so, she felt stiff. She rubbed at both wrists, working the feeling into her hands. She was fighting against the pins and needles, getting the better of her.

Behind her, she heard the chuckling again, rumbling impossibly through the sound deadened room. She turned to look, her upper body now free to twist in the seat, but she couldn't see anything except for more bones, though she noticed some of these were not as well picked as those closer to her. Some had flesh and meat still clinging to the bone. She could see the claw marks of where much of it had been torn away by small creatures.

"Don't worry, it's not the eating of your flesh that I hunger for. I enjoy... other carnal desires."

That voice rumbled through the room again, unnatural as it spoke, and still no sign of where it came from.

I wonder if he has a speaker somewhere. He's probably trying to fuck with me. That's what he wants, right? For me to be a character in his book. He wasn't liking the kidnapping writer, so he wants a book about demons now? Why can't he just make up his fucking mind?

"Hey, asshole, your book's a little lame. Writing about demons again? You've already done demons. How about something more original?" She yelled to the empty room, but if she was right, he had a speaker as well as a camera and microphone so he could watch and hear everything she did.

"Come on, you pervert. Come and get me."

The lights in the room flickered and then went out, casting the room again into darkness.

She could hear the bones shifting on the floor, and her ass clenched up. She held her breath, trying to force herself to see into that black ink of air around her. It was useless. It was as good as her having her eyes closed.

Her imagination ran wild as the bones continued to scrape and shift. She could picture them in her mind's eye, pulling themselves together, skeletons were rising up and finding the missing pieces from their bodies, forming into an army that was getting ready to surround her, tear into her and rip her apart. They wanted her flesh; they wanted to steal it from her bones to replace what they had lost. They were going to fight her for it.

If you ever get out of this, you are done reading horror novels, she told herself as she turned in the chair, trying to listen for when one of those skeletons would get close to her.

Then the bones started shattering. It was like they were exploding, and she could hear the dust as they disintegrated and rained down behind her. The sound of something large taking a heavy step preceded the destruction, crushing bone, but it didn't sound right. The foot, it wasn't like what she would expect, but it was familiar. She couldn't quite place where she knew that sound from. It wasn't a foot or a shoe, though. It was harder than that, a sharper sound that carried with it a little echo which should have been impossible in the room. Could have been a boot, a cowboy boot with those hard soles, but she didn't think that was right either.

There was a low, rumbling chuckle from the shape moving behind her.

The footsteps stopped.

The room fell deafening silent again. The only sound was that of her breathing.

She could feel it getting stifling hot. So far, it had only grown intensely cold, but now the room felt like it was on fire. She could imagine feeling invisible flames racing towards her.

Fuck this!

Lexi bent forward and felt with her hands down her legs until she found the two restraints that were wrapped around her ankles. The clasps felt similar to her wrists and, using both hands on each, she was able to quickly free herself. She didn't know where she was going or what the hell she was going to do, but she was getting the hell out of there.

She leaned back, getting ready to get out of the chair.

The light came back on and within an inch from the tip of her nose, a large, black face loomed. She couldn't make out its features because she was focused on the big orange eyes of raging fire that burned into her own, and the mouth of long, fanged teeth opened in a wide smile that sent shivers to her core.

A long, forked tongue emerged from its mouth and it ran along its upper lip as it hovered there.

Lexi tried to get away from it, to pull herself back against the chair as far as possible. She would melt into it and become one with it if she could. She turned her head to the side just to get an extra couple of inches of distance.

It only moved closer, slowly creeping in until it flicked that long tongue out and ran it up her cheek.

"Have fun. I know I will," the thing said, though she never saw that large mouth actually move, but yet she knew it came from it.

Then it was gone.

The room was empty, and she was alone again with the only sound being her. Though this time, her breath came in rapid succession as she struggled to get it under control.

CHAPTER 12

Fuck this shit. Lexi was done with this bullshit. It was time to find a way out.

She doubted there was another way to escape besides the door, so her only option was when the writer came to visit her next. She needed to stop being a character in his story. It was time that she took over the plot.

She stood, or more accurately, she attempted to stand. Her legs trembled and refused to hold her weight on her first attempt, and she crashed back into the chair. She caught herself, took a settling breath and again attempted to stand.

A stabbing pain sliced into her left rib, and she gasped for breath. That was a mistake, making it worse. Just breathing made it feel like a knife was piercing deep into her side, but when she looked, there was nothing there, no knives sticking out from her.

Damn it, she's had this before.

Short breaths. Try to relax, don't let it work its way in. Short breaths. You got this. You can do this. We just have to keep our head, and we'll get out of here.

She had looked into it before when she used to get stabbing pains in her side more often. Her Google searches had been scary and only made them worse for a while, but she realized where they had to be coming from. It was one of the most common causes of stabbing side pain.

Anxiety, the quiet killer. It had a way of paralyzing her, sometimes making it nearly impossible for her to get out of bed. Other times, like now, it would stab into her side and make it feel like anytime she breathed, a rib was about to spear through her lungs. It would go away, though; she just needed to sit there and take short breaths. Eventually, the pain would fade.

Do you really have time to just sit here? He could be back any minute and who knows what the hell that other thing was? Was that a hallucination?

It had to be. The other explanation was ludicrous.

Demons... A demon. Max. Isn't that what he called his demon in the book, too? The book she had read and done one of her video reviews on...

Just how much of this is actually real? Or maybe he did have a speaker hidden somewhere.

Lexi wouldn't have thought having the questions spin through her mind would comfort her, but somehow, it did. Just being able to string thoughts together was enough that she could feel the panic loosening its grip. She began taking experimental deeper breaths, at first unsure if it was too soon. She feared with any deep breath, the sharp pressure against her lungs would return.

After a few minutes, when she was sure she was past it, she straightened in the chair and looked at the door. For a second, she was sure she was going to see the large, black demonic shape looming over her, but felt a weight lift off her chest when nothing was there.

Lexi eased out of the chair, this time using the armrests to finish pushing herself up. Once on her feet, she used them again as support as she stood there, letting her legs tremble from the effort as she debated her next move. No matter what, she was not going to sit back down. It was time she worked on getting herself the hell out of there.

She looked around the room as she was now able to take it completely in. There wasn't much. The chair was centered and only an arm's length away from the door. That was good, as she didn't trust herself not to fall if she wasn't able to lean on something. It sucked, though, as there was no place to hide.

Hiding wouldn't have done her any good. He's already watching. He would have seen.

Everything she was doing, he would see.

Well, too bad. He was just going to have to deal with it. He was going to have to deal with her.

All she had was the chair and bones. The chair was fastened to the floor, but the bones...what could she do with the bones?

The wall, get moving, stay moving, and get the circulation back into your legs.

She knew she had to do it and reached out. Then, with a step closer to it, she let herself fall against the dark shapes that coned out from it. The dark cones that looked hard and firm while she was sitting down now seemed softer. They had to have been made from foam as there was give in them when she pressed.

She stopped herself from getting caught up in examining the structure that comprised the wall and ran her feet over the bones immediately around her. She wanted either a big, thick one that would make a good club or one that ended in a point that she could stab with.

She wasn't seeing any directly around her and forced herself to take a step to her right. It was actually good having the wall be so uneven. While she couldn't lean against it like she wanted, it gave her more objects to grab and use to support herself. Though she had to be careful, as there was still a point at the tip of the foam, even if it wasn't sharp.

Her mouth was so damn dry. Any benefit she gained from the little moisture offered by her own blood was gone, and she just wanted to drink anything. She hurt. She was sure she smelled, but by this point, she was so used to all the foulness in the air that she couldn't tell. As she took another stumbling step, this time making it to the wall's corner, she was hoping she'd see something she could drink just as much as finding anything she could use as a weapon.

Get yourself out of here, then we'll get a drink, she told herself as she scanned the bones beneath her. Still, she wasn't finding any that were sharp. There were ribs, but they were all from small animals. She figured they'd be too small and brittle. They would probably snap before breaking skin. Though if it came to it, she knew she'd try. After all, she could go for his eyes.

Which wasn't a bad idea, she thought as she made her way to the back. She could feel her legs gaining some strength as she moved. They didn't tremble as much, but she still didn't fully trust them.

As she got to where she could see more of the floor behind the chair, she saw that there was a pile of bones in the far corner away from her. It also appeared to be the "freshest" of them, as many of those were not rotted away. There was one skull that was half bashed in, but what remained still had parts of flesh that led Lexi to believe it had once been a young woman about her age. That skull, that severed head, it could have been her.

No, that could still become her if she didn't find a way out of there. She had to find some kind of weapon.

She made the turn to follow behind the chair and realized that the back wall was not equal distance. The top portion of the wall was farther back, like there was a shelf there, one long shelf that ran the width of the room. Because it was all painted black, the poor lighting and those cones all melded together into the optical illusion that it had been flat.

She wasn't sure if that was important or not, but it made it easier as now she had a clear place she could lean on as she shuffled her way to the pile in the corner.

92

Motion ahead of her made her stop. Something shifted on its own and a severed hand with fresh teeth marks in its palms slipped down until it rested on the crook of the young woman's nose, or what was left of it. It shifted the skull so that her one remaining eye turned toward her.

Lexi's heart skipped a beat when she swore she saw the woman blink at her with those lifeless grey eyes.

Lexi stood there motionless, holding her breath as she listened to the quiet in the room. As she adjusted to the impending silence, she could hear something. It had been imperceptible before, but now that she wasn't moving or breathing, she could make out the sound. There was something shifting around in that pile.

Lexi looked at the teeth marks on the palm of the exposed hand.

Fuck! Rats! She fucking hated rats. They were nasty and disgusting. Why was there a rat down here?

She wanted to back away and get away from the thing.

However, her stomach groaned, gurgling loudly in the room and reminding her just how hungry she was.

Would she really eat a rat, though?

She thought about the blood, how it twisted her insides, but she felt so good afterwards. This wouldn't be her own bodily fluids. This was fresh. It was food. It was blood; it was water, or the next closest thing she had available.

It was life.

Lexi found herself using the shelf next to her to lower herself down to her knees. Her legs trembled. She worried she was going to fall more than ease herself down, but she was able to do it. There was a small clearing in the bones, and she was able to kneel into it, trying not to disturb anything around her.

Good, stay quiet. Time to sneak up on the little bugger.

She was a couple feet away and shuffled her way forward. It could be heard on the cement, but she moved whatever bones were in her way gently off to the side. She was trying to make as little noise as possible.

The mound of bones shifted again, ever so slightly, and part of a rib cage slithered down. It bumped into the head, and then both of them continued in a mini body part avalanche. It cleared more bones from the pile, and her furry visitor was there looking back at her.

The rat sat up on its hind legs, now fully exposed, its beady eyes locked onto her own.

She didn't wait for it to decide what to do. Lexi lunged forward, putting everything she had to reach out and grab the rodent. She had started with her arms open wide, closing them fast as she came down with no regard for how she landed.

She was too slow, too hungry and exhausted as the rat was able to quickly scurry away from her. It disappeared into a dark shadow in the wall. She didn't fare as well, feeling it as soon as she came down. That stabbing pain in her side, much like she had felt earlier, tearing at her. Though this time she didn't think it was just anxiety that was making it hard for her to breathe.

She tried to roll to her right, away from the stabbing in her side, but the slightest twist sent waves of agony rippling through her body.

Shallow breaths. Shallow breaths, she told herself as she maneuvered onto her side. She could feel her shirt sticking to her as she did. That wasn't good, and she chanced a look down. Was there that much blood before? She knew when she'd knelt on the floor, it hadn't been wet and covered in it. If there had been a pool, she would have been lapping it up like a dog. She was so damned thirsty.

No, that wasn't right. It had to be coming from her.

Shallow breaths. Why is it getting so dark in here?

She was having a hard time twisting, but she finally did it. She could see something sticking out of her.

A bone? No, her bones should all be inside of her. She hadn't broken anything had she? Why was it getting so hard to think? None of that made sense. Her bones weren't broken.

Something sharp. She had been looking for a sharp bone to use as a weapon.

The wheels spun; thoughts were on the edge of making sense. Something about looking for a sharp bone, while another part of her was laughing at herself, telling her she had found a sharp bone after all.

No, that couldn't be a bone stabbing into her. She would have felt it, wouldn't she?

She had felt it. She thought it was a little high for that stabbing pain she'd felt earlier.

But she could see it now, the rib bone that must have been protruding from the torso's chest. It had been partly snapped off, or must have been, as it was now lodged in her chest, pulled completely free from the torso she had fallen onto.

Short breaths. Keep with the short breaths.

The light was fading. It was harder to breathe those quick, ragged breaths, and she was questioning why she was even doing it.

She heard the door lock release, and it scraped open. It was behind her. She couldn't see him as he came into the room, but he moved to stand over her.

"This is disappointing."

"Fuck...you," she tried to say, but she doubted he could even hear it, as it was faint in her own ears.

"I guess you're not my main character after all. I guess I'm going to have to give your friend a visit. What was her name? Was it Amanda or Alexa? Something like that. She had reached out to me. Did I tell you that? She's really looking forward to some book mail from the author. She's wanting signed copies. She gave me her address and everything."

Jacob squatted down close to her, but she could barely see him in the fading light. Her breath was coming in shallower gasps and the time between grew distant.

"I don't want to disappoint her after all. Book mail is the best mail."

Jacob stood over Lexi as she struggled for her final breath. Lexi tried to fight it, but could feel herself slipping away.

"Too bad. I liked her. Really thought she had final girl potential."

MISSING PERSONS: LEXI PEABODY
VIDEO EXCERPT

Hey Flix fam. Lexi here and I'm going to get real with you. I'm not feeling too sexy tonight. I'm not doing too well. My mom is having one of her episodes. She was crying and telling me how she's been a terrible mom and how she's ruined me. Then she went off, telling me she doesn't deserve me and all this.

But then she goes on talking about she doesn't want to be here anymore. She's tired of being in pain all the time and tired of life and how she's ruining it for everyone. She thinks everyone just wants her to go off and die.

I mean, I get depression and feeling sorry for yourself. It's not easy, but see, well...

Okay, so my mom is saying all this, and I've had friends tell me she's just talking and that this is all nothing to worry about. My aunts and uncles all just feel like this is normal for her.

What none of them understand is that she's tried to kill herself before. She didn't get committed or anything. She told the hospital that it was a mistake that she took all those pills and walked off into suburbia to get lost just by accident. It had nothing to do with my dad dying and how defeated she felt, or how she told me I was the light of her eye, her little angel, and that I'd be better off without her.

So, look, she's done this before. So how am I supposed to feel when she starts telling me she doesn't want to live anymore? How am I supposed to take that? How am I supposed to cope? How do I write it off as nothing?

And the worst part is, sometimes I wish she would just do it and get it over with. I love her so much, but I'm so tired of this up and down, it's like I'm always emotionally being pulled around. What am I supposed to do? How am I supposed to live my life?

Am I a terrible daughter for thinking that...?

I love her so much; I don't want to lose her. I have her and I have my best friend. Outside of that, I don't have anyone in my life. Well, I have you guys, but you know what I mean?

I need her. I don't know how to be me without her. What would I ever do if I didn't have her to call? Sure as hell not my step-ahole...

I know I'm a crying mess tonight. Thank you all for listening to me.

Lexinotsosexy telling everyone to have a great night.

It's okay. I'll be fine. I'm always fine.

CHAPTER 13

Amanda set down her phone, her chest heavy and wetness just touching the corner of her eyes. She just watched one of Lexi's last videos. There was so much of her friend posted online. Sure, there were the camera-ready videos where much of it was staged for the most views, but there were also the real moments. Lexi loved to put on a show, but she'd also never been afraid to open up and let the world in to see the real her.

Amanda didn't know how she did it. That kind of openness just wasn't her. She tried to make videos like Lexi did, but often she stumbled over her words and was uncomfortable talking into her phone. It wasn't that people would be watching. She could never remember what she wanted to say. She'd start talking and then forget everything.

Lexi always knew what to say.

Amanda found another of Lexi's videos and pressed play. This time it wasn't a Skulz book review but for another horror author. Some Texas indie writer that she'd heard about who also wrote a lot of poetry. Lexi really liked his book, saying that it really moved her.

Lexi always loved her books. She loved talking about them and it showed once you got her going on the subject. Anything else and it would be short, curt answers, but if you asked her about a book, she could go on for the rest of the night. Amanda was surprised Lexi could keep her videos so short, considering.

There was a knock on Amanda's door and she dropped her phone in surprise. Why would someone be knocking on her door?

Could it be him?

Amanda felt her heart beating hard in her chest. She grabbed her phone from the floor as she stood, never taking her eyes off the door.

I should call that detective. She unlocked her phone, doing so as she quietly made her way across the room. She stepped carefully, trying not to bump into any of the piles of clothes or junk littered throughout the room. She needed to win the lottery so she could have someone come in and clean the damn place, she thought as she made it into the little hallway. To the right was the bathroom. In front of her was the only other door. This one led to her only entrance, or means of escape, depending on what happened.

She grabbed the taser as she passed the bathroom, then looked through the peephole. The detective was there.

Maybe she's found something?

Amanda quickly pulled open the door to see the detective looking at her, a nervous way about her as she looked around and bounced from foot to foot.

"Can I come in?"

"Do you want to go to the cafe again?"

"I'd rather speak to you inside. I have some news, but it's not good."

Amanda's heart sank, and she felt all her strength drain out of her. She didn't have the energy to go downstairs if she wanted to.

She stepped out of the way, opening a path for the detective to step into the small studio apartment. Once in, Amanda pointed to her desk chair while she herself sat on the edge of her fold-out couch bed. She could fold the bed back in for more seating, but one of the springs was broken, and it was more of a fight than it was worth to do so. It didn't matter; she didn't have guests over too often, anyway.

The detective didn't seem to notice the unpleasantness of her surroundings as she sat there, looking at her hands. There wasn't much light in the room, just a floor lamp next to the desk, and what light came in from the streetlamp from the street below. Amanda watched as the woman kept gripping and releasing her trembling hands.

What scared the police? Amanda wasn't sure, but she had to know. She needed to know what'd happened to her best friend.

"Have you found Lexi?" Amanda finally said, being unable to take the silence that had crept into the room. The detective looked at her, surprised, as though she just realized where she was.

"Lexi..." the detective trailed off again, looking out the open balcony door. She didn't turn back to Amanda, but finally continued on. "So, I contacted the FBI, and they looked into the author. They were going to interview him and get back to me this morning. I waited most the day before I called them this afternoon."

Detective Torrance looked back at Amanda, looked into her eyes. The detective seemed visibly confused for a moment.

"I called the officer I had talked to yesterday. His name was Hallorann. He was Agent Tim Hallorann, with two n's, I remember, as I thought that was an odd way to spell his name.

"Yesterday we had met. I explained everything, and he was going to drive up there himself to investigate. He couldn't do an amber alert, because your friend was over eighteen, but he was concerned when I told him about the writer. He even said that he'd heard of similar cases, but didn't know the statuses of those other investigations. He said he would have to check into it.

"So today I decided to call him this afternoon since he never called me..."

The detective's voice trailed off again, and Amanda swore she could see the mental fog rolling back in through her gray eyes.

The detective had gray eyes? She could have sworn they had been brown yesterday.

Detective Torrence looked back toward the balcony, and Amanda was afraid she'd lost her again. She wasn't sure what was wrong with the policewoman. She didn't remind her at all of the sharp, concerned detective she had met.

"What did Agent Hallorann say? When you called him, I mean."

"He didn't know who I was. Don't remember talking to me the day before or anything."

"Detective?"

The detective blinked again and again. It was like she was waking up, not fully realizing where she was.

"Sorry. I've just been so tired today. Didn't get much sleep last night. I kept having these nightmares. Not the normal stuff, at least. Where was I?"

"Agent Hallorann. You said he didn't remember you?"

"Yes. Isn't that strange? Didn't remember talking to the writer at all. Couldn't tell me what he did yesterday. His log showed that he went to Wisconsin, but he couldn't remember why.

"I asked him more about it and he hung up on me as though I was some country bumpkin. Don't you think that's weird?" the detective said, but her voice trailed off and this time, Amanda knew she wasn't imagining it as she watched. The detective's eyes were looking deep into her own and she clearly saw those brown eyes lighten, graying over before the detective turned to look away.

"Detective?" Amanda said, knowing she'd lost her again. She had slipped into that mental fog, dazed as she stared off into space. This time, though, she didn't break free when Amanda spoke to her. She just continued to sit there, zoning out.

Amanda wasn't sure what she should do. Should she shake the woman? That would require her to touch her, and right now, Amanda was afraid to get any closer to her. What would happen if she did?

"I was introduced, and we both started grooving," Detective Torrance started to say, but it was quiet, just above a whisper and spoken almost in a singsong way as she said it. "I feel summer creepin' in and I'm tired of this town again..."

Was she singing? Amanda could swear it sounded like the detective was singing, but it was so quiet that it was just above a breathy whisper. She was, though; she was singing. She was even swaying back and forth, her head moving in time to some beat Amanda couldn't hear.

"Take me as I come... take me as I come... Take me as I come, 'cause you won't be here for long..."

Detective Torrance's voice drifted off. Then she blinked and stood from the chair. Amanda was quick to follow suit but kept her distance. The detective may have woken up out of whatever trance she was in, but she could just as easily have not.

"Detective?" Amanda was feeling uncomfortable with how she kept repeating herself as she tried to pull the woman back.

"Oh, yeah, so I'm going to be leaving now," Detective Torrance said, though her voice was distant as she walked to the door. She didn't wait for Amanda as she reached out, opening it and walking out into the hallway.

Amanda rushed to keep up and before the detective could close the door, asked her, "So what do we do now?"

"Do now?"

"About finding Lexi?"

"Lexi who?"

Amanda nearly opened her mouth but saw that the grayness had returned to her eyes. Amanda didn't think she was talking to the detective anymore.

"Never mind."

There was a slight smile that never quite reached the detective's eyes as she nodded back.

Amanda closed the door and watched her through the peephole. The detective stayed there, looking back and forth down the apartment complex hallway. She looked lost, like she didn't know where she was. She looked everywhere, except for back at Amanda's door. It was like she was intentionally trying to avoid possibly meeting her gaze through the small looking glass.

Finally, the detective pulled out her phone, looked at it, then made her way towards the stairs. When she was fully out of view, Amanda stepped back from the door, unsure just what she should be doing now. Who do you call when everyone you've already gone to has been wiped clean?

This wasn't natural, and Amanda began to feel like there was something really wrong with her friend's disappearance. Like, this wasn't earthly, there was something truly strange with how this was all playing out.

This was almost like it had to be some kind of supernatural thing. Who do you go to for that? A priest? Ghostbusters? *Who ya gonna call?* All she knew was fiction.

Amanda was trying not to panic, but could feel herself slipping into the deep pit of another one of her anxiety attacks. She could feel it coming on, and the worse part was that even though she knew it was coming, there was nothing she could do to stop it. Once that train started, there was no getting off the rollercoaster until it had run its course.

She had nowhere to go. She had no one to call. She was trapped.

Then the power went out, and everything around her went black.

CHAPTER 14

Amanda quickly turned around, taking in her room, looking for any light, anything that would allow her to guide herself. She needed to get somewhere safe, somewhere she could sit until the power came back on. Unfortunately, her little apartment was such a mess. Navigating it without a light could be hazardous to your health. Even she didn't feel confident she could make it to her bed if she had absolutely nothing to guide her.

There was a crisp gust of air that caressed the nape of her neck. It caused a ripple of cold to slither down her spine.

She remembered her door was unlocked and locked it. It gave her time as she let her eyes adjust to the darkness before she turned around.

Thankfully, there was a little light from outside that came in through the balcony window, but not much. It was just enough to make out shapes to avoid, but she would have to feel something to determine if it was the garbage can, clothes, or a random pile of books from one of her many TBR piles.

She made her way to her bed and, more importantly, found her way to the large, plush bean bag chair she kept in the corner. With the power out, it seemed like the perfect time to sit and watch outside while she thought about everything.

She felt tired, drained, riled up and frustrated, the conflicting emotions coursing through her, putting her on edge. Her body was electric to the point where she thought she could feel her teeth tingling with anticipation. She wanted to do something but didn't know what.

Think first. What the hell is going on? What the hell was that with the detective? It was clear that whatever happened to the FBI had also happened to the police.

What does that mean for her?

She watched the street outside. The streetlight was on, so it was just her building without power. Not the first time since she'd moved there. It was an old building, so someone probably blew a fuse. It was one of the curses of not having to pay a power bill.

Who? Who could she turn to?

Her phone lit up with a notification from where she'd left it on the bedside table. She didn't catch what it was before it faded back into her lock screen, but her gaze lingered on the phone.

She didn't have a lot of followers, but that didn't really matter. Followers or not, it was up to the algorithm, not follower count for a video to be seen...

She grabbed her phone and opened the Flix app, going right away to the "LIVE" icon on the screen. She'd never done a live before and felt nervous as the screen started flashing, counting down from five. On the screen behind the numbers, she could just see herself, her face dark, and the room darker behind her. If not for the little glow from her phone, she would probably have been lost to the background.

The countdown reached one, then a large 'Start' flashed and a counter on the side of the screen told her how many people were watching her. So far, the counter read "0".

"Hey everyone, or I guess, hey Flix fam, as Lexi would always say. So, many of you probably don't really know who I am, but my best friend was Lexi. You knew her as LexiSexyReads as she always liked to make videos, whether it be corny stuff with me in the background, or book reviews. People really seemed to like her book reviews."

Counter – 1
Leroy has joined this live.

"Hey Leroy. So, as I said, I was friends with Lexi. Something is going on. Something strange is happening, and well, I really need some help because I don't know what to do."

Counter – 3
JSHorrorsby has joined this live

"Lexi's gone. She *was* kidnapped, killed, I don't know, and I don't know what to do."

Leroy in chat:

Call the cops.

"I tried that. I called the cops," Amanda said, looking up from her phone and taking in her room. Not to look there, but as she couldn't bring herself to keep her eyes locked on her phone.

Counter – 10
Tinsletown has joined the live

"I called the cops, and that's where it gets really weird." Amanda sniffed as her sinuses were beginning to threaten to run and she wished she brought over a tissue before she started the live. She could see in her reflection her face

109

was starting to sparkle, light glinting off the tears that were streaking down her cheeks.

Damn it, I really didn't want to cry on this...

TinaB1 in chat:
What do you mean by weird?

"So, the detective just left my apartment. She told me she called the FBI, and they went to check out the person who took her. I know he took her, and they went to talk to him. Okay?

"She called the FBI today to get an update, and the FBI didn't ever remember talking to her. File's gone. Still shows that they went to his place yesterday, well, it shows they went somewhere in Wisconsin, but they don't remember going or why."

Leroy in chat:
Woah

Counter – 25
SJ Mass has joined the live.

BMatson – Horrorflix in chat:
What is this? This some kind of prank?

Tonedead in chat:
That's bullshit.

SJ Mass in chat:
Is this some kind of horror stream?

"I'm not making this up. My friend is missing. She was last seen meeting with-" Amanda's phone screen glitched and she blinked with surprise, staring at the black screen. Then it came back, and she was still in her live session.

110

"That was the last time anyone saw her. The FBI went and checked him out, but now the detective just left, and I kid you not. I swear she forgot as well."

JeffZ – Horror Author in chat:
People don't just forget missing people. Your friend is probably staying with someone. Who did you say she met? They are probably hanging around together, and you're making a big deal over nothing.

"Thanks. No, I know he took her. You're as bad as her stepdad."

TomTom in chat:
Stepdad, huh? She probably did run away.

MeganLosttoRead in chat:
I'm sorry about your friend. What did the detective say? What happened to her?

UnicornKiller in chat:
What's going on? What is this?

"It's not what the detective said so much as much as how she acted. I saw her eyes go gray. They just faded out and she kept forgetting what she was talking about. It was weird."

Tonedef in chat:
Sounds like you have a great police department there. What kind of drugs are they on?

UnicornKiller in chat:
Is this some kind of story? Cool horror vibe with the dark room.

"I don't think she was on drugs. I talked to her yesterday, and she was really professional and even started the investigation before the official twenty-four hours were up. Look, I think something supernatural is going on, and I need people to tell me what I should do."

MrWilly in chat:
Why supernatural?

"Because when I tried to show her the address for the person who took her, my phone blurred out. Any time she tried to look at anything belong to ----- It blurred out?"

MrWilly in chat:
To who? Your voice dropped out.

Counter – 666
Tomas has joined the live

"Really? You didn't hear when I said -----."

MrWilly in Chat:
Nothing. Voice dropped again.

UnicornKiller in chat:
Bruh, what's up with that demon mask in the background? Amazing burning eyes. Is that some kind of filter?

JSHorrorsby in chat:
Are you ready to join your friend?

MrWilly in chat:
I don't think that's a filter.

MrWilly in chat:
I think you need to get out of there. I'm sending you a DM. We need to talk. I think you are being possessed by a-

UnicornKiller in chat:
That is so cool. How do you get its eyes to glow like that?

"What do you mean? What glowing eyes?" Amanda said, looking at her reflection on the screen, though she hadn't noticed it before as she had been fixated on the text scrolling along. It did look like there could be a face behind her, with two glowing eyes.

Her heart raced as she gripped her phone tighter in her hand.

Gabs123 in chat:
That is a wicked effect. What filter is that?

"I'm not using any filters," Amanda said as she turned to look behind her. She moved slowly, not wanting to see what was there.

But there was nothing. Just her corner where two unpainted, unflattering white walls joined.

Amanda looked back at the phone and no longer saw the face behind her or the glowing orbs. She scrolled up to see what she missed in the chat.

UnicornKiller in chat:
Woah, where'd it go?

MeganLovestoRead in chat:
Are you okay?

MrWilly in chat:
You need to get out of there. Get to sanctified ground. Is there a church nearby?

JSHorrorsby in chat:
He's watching you. He wants your soul.

SJ Mass in chat:
Get out of here, troll. Can't you see she's upset?

"What do you mean I'm possessed? I know what I'm talking about. My friend is missing. It's not me," Amanda said, looking at her own terrified face in the screen.

MrWilly in chat:
That looked like a demon. Demons either possess or they devour souls. You need to get away from it. You need to get somewhere safe.

UnicornKiller in chat:
Bruh, what are you talking about? It's just a filter effect.

MeganLovestoRead in chat:
You're upsetting her.

Gabs123 in chat:
Where would you even go for sanctified ground? It's not like churches would be open this late.

MeganLovestoRead in chat:
They have shelters nearby, don't they?

JSHorrorsby has liked this live.
UnicornKiller has liked this live.

MaryLisaFlix in chat:
Why are you guys liking this? She's terrified.

Amanda felt something cold tickle at the back of her neck before caressing down her back. It was like fingers of ice walking their way down her spine.

A tear worked its way free and fell onto her phone screen. She wiped it away and then wiped the tears on her face.

TomeWalker in chat:
Sanctified ground wouldn't work. There's no place for her to go. She has to fight the demon spiritually.

MrWilly in chat:
How would you know? Have you fought one?

TomeWalker in chat:
I have. Demons have no dominion in the physical realm. They are constructs conjured by man and subject to obey. Going to a church is not the answer.

Another cold gust came from behind her, but this time she noticed that none of the curtains by the balcony door moved.

She looked at her phone, getting closer to her screen to have a better look at what was behind her. She wasn't sure, but she thought she could see the outline of a face, something dark against the white walls behind her.

MrWilly in chat:
You need to get out of there.

UnicornKiller in chat:
Why can't we see its eyes?

JSHorrorsby in chat:
It's already too late.

MeganLovestoRead in chat:
Run.

MrWilly in chat:
Get somewhere safe. If not sanctified ground, get somewhere with lights, power and people. Get out of there.

TomeWalker in chat:
You need to call your priest. They will know how. They can pray with you.

"I don't have anywhere to go," Amanda sobbed, watching the face fill in behind her.

TomeWalker in chat:
Find God. God will always give you somewhere to go.

MrWilly in chat:
Get out of there now.

Gabs123 in chat:
Someone call the police. What's your address?

UnicornKiller in chat:
That isn't the same face as before.

Amanda stopped watching the screen scroll. She was getting too caught up in watching her own demise being live-streamed and needed to pull herself back to reality. What had MrWilly said? To run, find somewhere safe, somewhere sanctified. But just where was she going to go?

She could only think of one place she could get to easily, but that was crazy.

Amanda turned on the flashlight on her phone, and without looking behind her, navigated across the room and rushed through the door. She didn't worry about closing it or locking it as she burst into the hallway. Not once did she look at the man as he emerged from the shadows. His smile widened as he watched her run.

"Let's see if she can be my main character..." he said to the empty room. In the darkness, there was a low rumbling growl that faded as it moved to go after the girl.

MISSING PERSONS: LEXI PEABODY
VIDEO EXCERPT

Hey Flix fam, LexiSexy here and I know you want a book review. You know I've got one, but I just want to give a shout out to my BFF. You see her name there on the screen, click and give her some follows. She's an amazing person, even if I've sucked at being a bestie lately.

It's not my fault, A!

For those that don't know, I've started dating someone, and she's awesome. Bummer part is A and I not having the time to hang, but I promise, this weekend, it's you and me, coffee and books. I swear.

So, everyone, I did find an older Skulzy novel, but I tell you what, I'm beginning to notice he had a thing for demons. Seems like all his books in the last five years have one. It's like he's got a hard-on for them. Or the demons have a hard-on for him.

Sorry, not my best joke, but does lead into this book. This one is about a demon who traps a woman inside a mirror where she fights to get out, but while she's trapped there, there are these snake-like creatures that keep coming out of objects, chasing after her.

They come out of everywhere. There was one time they came out of the kitchen sink, then there were the little ones that came out of the outlets.

And she's in this prison world where it's like eternal night, and she's in the mirror so she can only see her husband on the other side who never sees her. She can only watch as he does his own sick stuff. He starts cheating on her and seems to have a fetish for bringing them back to their bedroom, where she is forced to watch.

It all finally builds to where Robyn is watching her husband choke the latest mistress, and she is pounding on the glass, trying to get his attention so the woman can get away. Robyn isn't paying attention when one of these snakes bite her. She kills it but then gets sick.

The book ends with one coming out of her lady bits and eating her. What the hell!

Oh shit, guess I gave that one away. Sorry, guys. I'm sorry, I've had a rough week, not getting a lot of sleep. I'll do better. No more ruined endings. I swear.

Book was called Inside the Mirrors. Night all and stay sexy everyone. LexiSexy is out, and I gotta date.

CHAPTER 15

The darkness was suffocating.

She was cut off from all the light in the world and squeezed into the tightness of her surroundings. She could only wiggle to move. The walls of the tunnel barely accommodated her body, her shoulder pushed against the slime-drenched surface she had stuffed herself into.

Yet she continued. The grime and slime of whatever lathered the walls helped her, but was also bile inducing in its stench. The odor assaulted her nostrils. She thought she was done being disgusted by the smells she associated with this hell, but it kept finding new ways to make her sick...

When Lexi woke, she was surprised to find that she was still alive. Her side still hurt, and she had no clue how much blood she had lost. It seemed like a lot, and she'd been woozy enough that she made no attempt to stand. She didn't trust that she would be able to, as just the effort it had taken to push herself onto her elbows had her trembling.

Still, Lexi had to find a way out of there. She had to keep shuffling forward. There was something she wasn't sure she saw, or if it had been a trick of the light. She couldn't imagine how deflated she'd feel if it was only a shadow cast on the wall, but if it wasn't... Maybe that was why there was pile of bones. Had others found nothing and gave up there? Or maybe he piled those bodies here as a way to hide something that he didn't want anyone to find.

Lexi felt a flash of quickly dissipating excitement as she cleared away the carcasses and could see it. There was an opening. It was small, but it was a chance for her to get out of there.

That chance became much slimmer when she fully reached the hole. There was a brownish green goo oozing out of it with stages of it having dried and crusted at the edge. The putrid stench that wafted out of it in droves caused her insides to recoil, but she tried to muster the willpower not to back away. This was her only way out, but just having to touch the disgusting substance was enough to twist her stomach into knots.

A series of dry heaves rampaged her and left her shaking. She didn't know if she even had the energy to crawl into it. Her arms felt like they were going to give out and she nearly crashed into the corpse beneath her.

Don't look down, do not look at it. She had been trying to avoid looking at the body she was on top of, as she didn't want to look at the disfigured face. What she had seen when climbing over it had been half the face ripped away, an eyeball squashed, gore running down the corpse's cheek where skin had been down to bone.

Oh god, oh god, oh god, just let me get out of here. She needed to do it. If she didn't make it now, there would be no escape. If they realized she was still alive, they would finish her off. The proof of that was literally below her. She had her hands on it, rubbery flesh cold to the touch sliding from the bone beneath as she tried to push off from it.

You can do this. You have to do this.

She held her breath and eased herself forward into the hole, only to find she didn't fit. She knew it looked tiny, but had not realized just how small until she wasn't able to fit the first time. It was narrower than the width of her shoulders by what felt like just less than half an inch.

Her only way to escape and she was too big to slip into it...

Maybe that was why all the bones were there. This was where the others had crawled to and had died not being able to get out. What had the others done to themselves to try to fit into the little hole? Just how many of the broken bones beneath her were from self-mutilation?

She let out the breath she had previously held and scrunched in her shoulders as close as she could, shooting herself forward, pushing herself like a torpedo being loaded into a tube with her legs pushing behind her. It was more energy than she thought she had, but she pushed herself in.

She fit into the darkness, and kept pushing until her legs couldn't push herself further.

Okay, now what? she thought as she made her first gasp to breathe. There was so little room that she could not take in much air, as to do so made the tube too tight and she found her chest again hitting hard cement, only softened by whatever ooze it was that she displaced. It wrapped itself around her, its cold, gel-like texture slithering like it had a life of its own as it moved within her crevices.

She had to keep moving, but there was nothing to grab onto, and her feet weren't even fully into the shaft yet. If that thing or Jacob found her like this, they could easily pull her back into their torture chamber, though she doubted they would do it quickly. She could imagine them chopping off her feet to start, pulling her out some, chopping off her legs at her knees, pulling out some more, before doing other things to her, things she refused to imagine, things she didn't want to think about.

Be a worm, slither, move your little fat ass, twist those shoulders and do this. Come on, you bitch, do this. She needed to do this. She had to find a way.

So, she slithered. She shook herself back and forth and she kept going. Even though it didn't feel like she was getting anywhere, she realized she had when she felt her feet were fully inside the tunnel. Then she could start using her toes as best she could to push herself by little segments.

It was hard work, and she didn't know how long she had been doing it for. She was in complete darkness and had no clue just when she would ever find an end. No matter how she tried to adjust to the black that was around her, hoping that she could see something with some kind of night vision, there was nothing to see. There was not even a trace of light to give her any sense of how far she needed to go or where this tunnel went to.

At least she had to be beyond reaching distance for if they found her now. She had to have been doing this long enough for that. She wasn't sure how long this would take, or how far she could go before she passed out or died, but at least she was beyond their reach.

What if that slithering thing came after her? It slithered up her leg while she was in the chair. What if they sent it? Had it even been real, though?

What if she wasn't the first to have tried escaping through there? What if she came upon something dead, or something to block her way?

Stop it. Focus on the tunnel and keep going. Stop it.

But when all you see is darkness, it is hard not to see monsters in the space you cannot see. Not after a lifetime exposed to the many creature features and Rosemary's Babies that fed imagination. We are not born with a fear of the dark; it is something that manifests, being crafted by the tales we consume.

And she had consumed many of them. Right now, she wished she could do without a few of them dancing through her imagination, waving its wand like a conductor leading an orchestra.

Her stomach grumbled, still a constant reminder of how long it had been since she had eaten.

She needed to get out of there. She just needed to make it until the end.

Even if it was the end that may never come, she needed to get some kind of release from this place. If that meant she died there, so be it. She had to keep moving until she felt death's icy touch rip her from this mortal world. She had to keep fighting. She wasn't going to give up, not like her mother found it so easy to do. She was never going to be like her, ever.

CHAPTER 16

Amanda escaped to the stairwell; the door slamming shut behind her as everything was still pitch black. Then a faint light glowed as her screen came back to life. She looked at it and saw she was still streaming, but could barely see her dark visage in the reflection.

UnicornKiller in chat:
Woah, you look like shit.

MrWilly in chat:
Don't stop. It's messing with you. Get out of there.

JSHorrorsby in chat:
I'm coming for you.

MeganLosttoRead in chat:
Someone report him.

JSHorrorsby in chat:
Hello Amanda, can I come in?

"How do you know my name?" Amanda said, her voice shaking as she tried to fight the terror that welled up inside her.

JSHorrorsby in chat:
I'm here for you, Amanda. It's time for you to be a part of the story.

No, no, no, no, NO! Amanda was screaming at herself as she quickly reached out, fumbling in the darkness to find the railing. It seemed farther than where it should have been, and her stomach lurched. What if it wasn't there anymore? What if she was in some void and she was going to reach forward and find herself falling into some merciless, unending pit?

She found the railing, but not by grabbing it. Her flailing hand flew up and the back of her wrist slammed into the metal hard enough that it rang out like a bell had been struck. The sound echoed down the stairwell, reverberating off the walls. She followed it with a howl of pain as she pulled her hand back to her chest, while making a mental note of where the railing had been.

Damn fool. Why don't you use the flashlight on your phone?

Because she was afraid to look back to the screen. She was afraid to see more messages from...him.

She had to look, but when she did, the screen was dark. She tapped on it, pressed the side button, and got no response. Her phone was dead.

There was no escape from the vast amount of nothingness around her. It messed with her mind, throwing her off balance as her equilibrium was interrupted by the absence of sight. She flexed her other hand as it throbbed with pain and lost focus as to where she had found the railing.

She stumbled and felt her legs grow weak, her knees shaking. She found herself stepping back, fearing her loss of balance and falling over into the unseen depths, however, her trembling legs gave in.

She fell hard, her butt crashing onto the cement floor, her upper back against the door. A nerve crushing pain shot down her lower back to her toes, which curled as her body seized from the shock. She didn't think she could move as the pain rippled up her thighs. Points that never made contact with the floor or the door screamed out in pain as her whole nervous system howled its complaint from her sudden landing.

She hurt. Oh, how she hurt more than she ever thought was possible. Everything felt damaged, but the throbbing pain in her wrist was the loudest in the symphony.

It was enough that for the few agonizing seconds of white-hot pain shooting through her wrist and back she forgot something was coming after her.

She was brought back to her new reality when something slammed into the door behind her. It pushed her forward before it slammed back into place. The man or thing didn't stop. It rebounded, hitting it again, over and over. Amanda quickly scrambled to get more of her body weight against the heavy metal door.

It was cold on her back, though she felt it getting warmer. Whatever was slamming into it growled in frustration, and she knew that it was not a man. She had tried to convince herself that it had been, but the roars vibrating through the metal from the other side were not human. She could hear its billowing breath before each new assault, quickly followed by the door shuddering. Each time it hit, there was that little gap before the door slammed back again, she could feel the rush of that hot breath as it wrapped around her. It reeked of sourness. It was the smell of bad meat and sulfur and every time she breathed it in, she had to bite down the vomit that threatened to choke her in the back of her throat, burning as it sat there wanting to escape.

"Come on, little girl, have some fun with me." It was more of a growl than a voice that spoke to her. The door rumbled with each word, but she could feel it tremble through her very soul. Her teeth clenched as she fought to keep it from getting into her mind. She felt its tendrils prying, and she struggled to push it away.

She needed to get out of there. How though? She couldn't leave the door, or it would be right on her.

On the other side, she heard scraping sounds as large claws ran slowly down. They were careful, moving with purpose, and if they wanted to tear through that metal, she had no doubt they could.

"Why? Why are you doing this?" She sobbed as she screamed at that scraping sound, the feeling of it grinding at her nerves. Though she knew why. She'd reached out. She had wanted to save her friend. All she wanted to do was save Lexi. She had no clue how wrong that had been.

It slammed into the door again; this time with the force to launch her into the air. Her stomach lurched with a sense of weightlessness, lost to darkness and the void, sure that she had been propelled high and far enough that she was going to fly over the security rail and into the great beyond of the stairwell. A fear that grew as she never landed. The darkness held her for what seemed much too long, and she only felt air rushing around her. She had no way of knowing where she was. She could be falling to her death at the bottom of the stairs and slam into concrete at any time.

But she never landed.

She was lost in nothing.

Time slipped away from her.

Then she did land. Amanda slammed back, pulled by some force that ripped her out of the air and brought her against the metal door. Her head slammed against it and even in the dark, she saw stars form at the corner of her vision that were quickly replaced by dancing, glowing snakes of light. She wished the light was real, but knew it was all just an illusion.

She struggled to find air, as it had been expelled out of her from the force. Her lungs ached as she fought to pull in oxygen. Shallow gasps were all she could do, as it felt like her body worked against her and refused more. Any deeper of a breath and it hurt. It felt like every gasp was ripping apart her insides.

When she was finally able to pull in slow, controlled breaths, the glowing snakes and the strain around her vision faded. She was left in the dark. The world was suddenly quiet except for the sound of her breathing, which was becoming loud in the silence. Though those labored breaths were in a sense its own comfort, as it was all that she heard.

Had the monster left? Was she alone?

As much as she wanted to open that door to check, she feared what she would find on the other side.

No, she needed to do what she had started. She was getting out of there. She needed to escape. She needed people. Find somewhere that there was a crowd, and she would be safe.

She didn't know where that was, or what safe looked like, but if it had stopped trying to get through that door, she needed to take the opportunity to get downstairs to the lobby.

She felt her way in the dark, moving her hands along the ground until she felt the first step down. Working her way up, she grabbed the rail and carefully continued to feel with her hands. Once she grabbed onto the cold metal, she never let go, instead sliding down its length. Each step she took carefully, her foot leaving one step and keeping it close to the back of the next until it landed. This way, she didn't have to worry about overreaching. She wasn't about to risk getting through all that just to go tumbling down to the bottom and breaking her neck.

She breathed a quick sigh of relief as she reached the lower platform. A platform that she knew within a few steps would lead to the door. She remembered that above it, there should have been an exit sign lighting the way.

Her stomach twisted at the realization that even that light was gone.

That's impossible.

Amanda felt her heart race in her chest as her lungs flared. What was this darkness? This wasn't natural. This wasn't a power outage.

You're just now figuring that out? You knew it wasn't natural. You knew it, you just refused to let yourself believe it because if it was a power outage, you could get away.

No, she was going to get away. She needed to-

Amanda rushed to where the door should have been. She thought she knew what she was getting into, but this was more than she had bargained for. It was supposed to be just some horror author who had kidnapped her friend. She meant to get his address, give it to the police, and have them go and save Lexi. She never planned for anything like this.

Maybe she could call that detective, and she would come and take her somewhere safe. She might not remember much, but maybe that wouldn't even matter.

Of course, that would mean her phone had to work. The screen was still black, an unseen object she had lost somewhere when she fell against the door above.

No, she needed to keep going, to get out of there and find somewhere, anywhere, that was safe. The first place she could think of was the coffee shop. They'd be open, and they were usually busy in the evenings thanks to indie artists that performed. She could go there for now while she figured out her next move.

Amanda slammed through the door, light immediately flooding her vision. It was so sudden that it blinded her, and she raised her hands to block it without even realizing what she was doing. It didn't matter how hard it was to see, and how her eyes were not adjusted to it. It was too

late. She could already see her mistake. She was not in the lobby...

CHAPTER 17

Lexi was awakened by a pain stabbing into the bottom of her foot. Something quick was making tiny jabs that were sharp and tearing into her flesh.

"Ah!" she screamed before she could catch herself from making too much noise and she tried to kick whatever was hurting her. In the process, she slammed her knee into the wall of the tunnel before bringing it down. The momentum was dulled, but she was still able to slam her foot down and felt the furry shape that it hit.

She took little satisfaction when it was knocked away from her foot, as the rat would not have been hurt that much. Her knee took most of the force in the tunnel wall, she didn't so much kick the rat as much as just pushed it away.

And it didn't work. Within seconds, the rat was back again and attacking where it had already torn into the bottom of her foot. It was vicious as it worked to tear away more skin and without being able to see it, she could only imagine watching as it took pieces of her flesh and ate out of its disgusting little claws, ingesting pieces of her as food.

No, fuck that.

Fuck being that things dinner. Fuck feeding its family, as she was sure there were more of them. She needed to get out of there, and for now, it meant taking out that disgusting nugget that she wished she could eat herself, because she was sure as hell hungry enough right now that she would do it.

The thought of grabbing the furry little beast and biting into its flesh, letting the blood run down her body as well as her throat, made her stomach growl with anticipation and hope. Her tongue, heavy with cottonmouth, ran the length of her teeth as she wanted nothing more at that second than to devour that vicious mother fucker.

It bit her foot again, bringing her out of her hunger dream, and she scissor-kicked and kept kicking. She couldn't get a lot of force into each blow, so she knew she had to kick fast and as much as possible. Her hope was to catch it between her feet and do some damage. She doubted she would be able to kill it, but if she could get it to run...

Her stomach rumbled again, and she could feel her mouth moisten. If only she could find a way to get at it. She wanted to feel that fur around her mouth as she ripped it away; the blood spurting down her face. She was so thirsty that the thought of drinking it, of drinking anything, was a blessing.

She stopped. She wasn't sure if she had been kicking the rat or her own feet. It was hard to know, as she hadn't been sure if she'd kicked anything furry in the last few moments.

She waited for it to start gnawing on her feet again, but nothing.

She needed to get out of this damn tunnel.

Now that she was awake again, unsure just when or how long ago she had drifted off, she started squirming again, trying to get to an exit. If not, then she would be left to rot there, nothing more than rat food, as they were the kings of this hell.

If there was one of them, then there were more of them. Who knew how long it would be before an army of them flooded this tunnel, their turn to take her as their prize?

She could see them in her mind's eye, swarming her body, eating through her to continue down the tunnel, tearing apart her flesh, eating their own path through her organs. *Come on, Lexi, keep going. You can do this.* She wished she could believe that, but nonetheless, she was not about to give up now.

* * * *

Lexi wasn't sure how long she had been slithering through the dark tunnel when she heard it. She stopped so she could listen because her grunts and squirming sounds made it hard to hear anything other than herself.

At first, she thought that maybe she had been mistaken. She had stopped moving and the noise she had thought she'd heard was no longer there. There was only her breathing and even that grew quiet as it slowed.

Mentally she started to count to a hundred, though as she neared forty, she could feel her eyelids growing heavy. At fifty-two, she thought she'd lost count, possibly drifting off. She resumed, but wasn't sure if she skipped a number or ten. At sixty, she thought she caught herself snorting awake and wasn't sure if she was at sixty or fifty. Had she left a couple of numbers out? She thought she skipped fifty-seven; she was always skipping fifty-seven anytime she had to count to a hundred and would often find herself starting over.

She never made it to seventy but woke with a start, thinking the number was where she was at in the count. It didn't matter, as she felt the fur of the creature she had been listening for as it rubbed against her nose. The rat had been quick, too fast for her to try to twist around and bite it. It had rubbed against her, but then it was gone to the darkness.

She listened, trying to hear whether it was scurrying around, checking her out, or if it was running away. She thought she heard it moving towards her right, but wasn't sure if it was real or what she wanted to hear.

She was done with the counting as she listened intently to her surroundings. Counting dulled her senses. She needed to be alert. It was still there somewhere in the dark. She could feel it. She sensed it getting closer.

The only thing you're feeling is your hunger. Your growling stomach is loud enough to scare away a bear, let alone some scared rat.

She found that she was grinding her teeth, trying to clamp down her growing need. She wished she had more room so that she could use her arms and reach out. Having them stuck to her side made it more frustrating knowing that it was out there.

The rat ran by her again; a silent ninja in the dark until she felt its fur bristle past her cheek. She quickly turned her head, launching herself the best she could, maybe moving half an inch, if she was lucky, in its direction as she tried to chomp down on its flesh. Her teeth were loud as they caught nothing but air and came down hard on her incisors.

In the dark, she swore she could hear the rat laughing at her, mocking her as she ground her teeth.

Then there was nothing but silence.

She waited, but she never felt its fur again. It had disappeared into the unseen. Or had it ever really been there? Like so much, she wasn't sure if any of this was real. Was she even really alive or was she trapped in some impossible limbo, in a test tube, a science experiment in the cosmic lab of life?

Her stomach growled, and she felt that sensation again, swimming in her own thoughts. The way the world swayed, even with the walls tight against her. Somehow it still felt like everything was unsteady and shifting, changing while she stayed there.

She tried to keep her thoughts together and stay focused on getting out of there, but with the world a constant unknown of reality or fiction, she wasn't sure what she was still fighting for.

Food, you're fighting for food. All she wanted was food. Right then, she would be just as happy to rip a rat apart as she would with a steak burger from Steak' n' Shake. Either way, food, drink, anything. She just needed something.

Even the slime around her felt like it might be a possibility, even if it was toxic and would probably kill her. Though she'd already tried. No matter how hard she shifted, it was always just out of reach for even her tongue to touch its surface. Which was odd, she would think she should be able to reach it, but somehow, she just couldn't.

Come on, you bitch. Keep shuffling. Don't give in to this shit. You've never let anyone get you down. Not your piece of shit stepfather, none of them. You've never let them stop you before. You're not about to let this asshole win. You got this; you are going to get out of here. Just keep moving. You are going to do this. You are going to do this. You are stronger than you think, and deep down, you know that. You've had your downs, but you have always gotten yourself back up. Come on. Keep moving. You just need to keep moving.

Lexi felt the tears try to leak from eye ducts that had dried long ago, because she recognized that voice in herself. She had fought it many times, when she was down and through her rough times, it always tried to get her motivated. Rarely did she listen. There were so many times that she'd wanted to give up. It was just so easy to think about giving in. After all, why was she trying so hard? What was out there for her to work towards?

The voice was always so hard to listen to, but she knew she had to. This time, if she did give up, it truly would be the end. She had to keep fighting. She had to get out of there. This tunnel had to lead somewhere.

Lexi took a moment to think about Jacob Skulz's books. She read all of them, at least she thought she had. Did any of them have a tunnel in them? Well, no, but none of them had a room full of bones in them before either.

So, was this a new house, or did he redesign?

This was meant to be something for her to get to, wasn't it? He wanted to write a story about her, so he had to have some place for her to go, but what was the story?

Skulz had acted like he didn't know, but of course, he wouldn't tell her. He'd want her to find it for herself, but that meant that there had to be a place for her to reach. She just had to get there.

What was she going to do when she did? No one lived in his stories. They were depressing; he didn't believe in happy endings. He even said as much in interviews. Horror books shouldn't have happy endings, or else they weren't really a good horror book. So, wherever this went to, it was meant to kill her. That was his game.

Wherever this led, when she got there, she needed to figure out what he had planned for her. She needed to find it, because if there was any way for her to survive, she had to turn the story around on him. She needed to take control of it.

Lexi realized that she must be nearing some form of light source, even though she couldn't see it, she could begin to make out the walls around her. It wasn't much, just an outline of the shifting of the slime as she worked her way through it. When she looked up, she could make out the glint of two eyes that were looking at her; the rat, as it watched her work her way closer to it.

It watched her before it turned around and ran away.

She continued worming her way toward it, and to whatever end she would find.

CHAPTER 18

Amanda found herself in the hallway upstairs. The lights were on, and behind her, the large metal door to the stairwell was untouched. There was no trace that there had ever been any monster trying to claw its way through to get to her.

To her left was her apartment door, slightly ajar from when she had run from it. The lights had been out; she wasn't sure if she closed it or not. She had been running for her life, not worried if someone was going to break into her place. What would they get anyway? Her Chromebook? Yeah, like that was worth much.

What was she going to do now?

She tried to catch her breath as she took in the quiet hallway. In all that running, yelling, everything that had just happened to her, no one had left their own apartment. Not a single person was even the slightest concerned about what was happening. That was odd.

She couldn't remember a time when Ms. Jensen wasn't popping her head out when she heard someone in the hall. She was the nosiest person Amanda had ever known, always in everyone's business. So where was she? She was an old lady on social security, so it's not like she had a job or anywhere to go. Watching the hall was probably the only thing she had to do all day.

Amanda thought about going the few doors down the hall and knocking to check on the old woman, but something twisted in her gut, telling her she shouldn't.

But why shouldn't you? It made sense. It was rational. You don't have your phone on you. You could knock on any of these doors and try to get help, maybe call that detective.

It did make sense. Why had she even thought of not doing it? While Ms. Jensen was nosy, she was also very kind. She would definitely let her use her phone. It was a landline; she doubted the woman would ever get a cell phone, so she'd had to dial the police through information. Ms. Jensen probably had the number. She could help her call.

Amanda took a few steps toward the old woman's door when the hallway shifted. She felt the floor moving under her feet and the walls around her stretched. It was fast, in a heartbeat, and before Amanda could comprehend just what was going on around her, she realized that all the doors were gone so that only hers remained. She had nowhere else to go.

No, you don't. Go back into the stairwell, get downstairs. You have to try again, but no matter what, you cannot go back in there. It's waiting for you there.

Amanda feared the voice was right, but when she looked behind her, she saw that the door to the stairs was gone as well. She only had one door to choose, and she was afraid of just what would happen if she stayed in the hallway.

She gently pushed open the door and saw that the light was back on in her apartment. She didn't see anything else that was off, except that her phone was on her bed. She could see the screen lit up, not sure what was still being shown.

It wanted you back here for a reason. Why?

She wasn't sure, but her gut told her not to cross the room for her phone. That wasn't where she left it when she ran out. She was sure she'd had it with her.

"Hello?" she said to the empty room and wasn't sure what she was waiting for in reply.

Standing there, she would have thought she was being silly, calling out to her quiet apartment, had she not been chased from it just a few minutes ago. The realization was heavily weighing on her, almost suffocating her. She had nowhere else to go, and she needed her phone. It was the only way she could call for help.

Who though? Who are you going to call?

She had to call Lexi's mom. She'd helped her before. She was the only one she could talk to about this. She was the only one who could help. Amanda just needed to get past Tee's stupid husband.

Amanda took a small step into the apartment and then another, waiting for something to jump out at her. The room had a chill to it that didn't seem right for these summer months, but she couldn't pinpoint the source. Her balcony door was open; the night sky ablaze with the city lights outside, but the curtains were still. There was no breeze justifying the frigid air.

She made her way to her phone and looked at her reflection on the screen. The live stream was still active, but there were no longer any viewers. She closed it and moved back through the room towards the door.

Nothing stopped her or reached out to her. The room was incredibly silent to the point that even the hum of the refrigerator was loud in her ears.

In the little hallway that led to her only way out, she allowed herself a moment of relief as she'd feared something grabbing her, reaching out from beneath the many piles of junk and clothes. Thankfully, she didn't read as many scary books as Lexi, so the reserve of creatures she could imagine coming after her was limited. That didn't mean something couldn't be there. It just meant she wasn't sure what might be lurking in the shadows.

She looked at her closet; the doors open wide due to childhood fears of closed doors. To her right was the door to the bathroom, also left open. The only door closed in the room was the one she needed. The only way she had to leave.

But what if there were no other doors out there again? Then where would she go?

She wasn't sure if she could leave. She didn't know if she was a prisoner in her own apartment or if it was just guiding her back in here for something. It felt like it was just messing with her, but it had to be pushing her somewhere.

You don't have any other options. You have to go out that door. Either that or stay in her little apartment for the rest of her life, which she didn't think would be for much longer.

She walked the length of the hallway and reached for the door. Just as she grabbed it, a black claw emerged from the door and wrapped around her hand. Its grip was firm and held it in place tight around the knob. The claw engulfed her hand, with each finger ending in a sharp talon. She could feel those talons digging in, threatening to break skin.

She screamed when the metal quickly became hot in her grip, and she could feel her flesh burning. She could smell it and saw smoke rising through the claw's fingers.

She tried to pull her hand away, but the grip was impossible to break. She dropped her phone and reached out with her other hand, trying to twist and pull her hand free. She frantically struggled to pry even just one of the black fingers away as the fire against her palm caused her skin to sizzle. The sound grew so loud that it had to mean the flesh was being scorched away from where it touched the metal of the knob.

A wind blew through the room, a frigid gust of air that was enough to bite through her flesh and attack her deep into her bones. It was cold. She could feel its chill, but as the wind blew, it mingled in her mind with the heat from her hand and it set ablaze all her nerve endings. Her mind registered the cold air, but it also felt like a white-hot fire was scorching through every part of her.

Amanda screamed, as she was sure she was burning alive; a modern-day witch being seared away at a stake for crimes she was unaware. She felt it continuing to assault her, until she hadn't even realized that the claw had released, and she found herself falling to the floor, her strength having abandoned her.

Her carpeting felt like she'd landed on a bed of nails, harsh against her raw skin.

It brought back the memory of her first time lying on it. She had just signed the lease, and it was her first place that was outside the roost of her parents' nest. She had come up there, didn't have any furniture with her, it was just her and her new place. She had gone in and laid down on that very carpeting and nestled herself into it. It was hers, and there had been a comfort in just lying there in what was now hers and hers alone. It was her first place, and she was finally free.

The carpet had lost that sense of comfort as each bristle felt like it was stabbing her. She twisted, but every change caused more contact with her raw skin. She got to her knees, but every time her palm came down, it was a fresh wave of fire that ignited as a reminder not to use that hand.

The wind seemed like it was swooping down on her with its most powerful gale, and she felt herself beginning to shake with the chills as they racked her body. She wasn't dressed for the freezing temperatures. It was summer, a hot summer, and she'd been in a simple V-neck shirt and her capris, not dressed to go out into the winter cold. It was something she'd never thought she would have to worry about in July, yet now she wished she had been live streaming in a parka and wearing her wool pajama pants.

Her skin no longer felt like it was on fire. She wished she could be relieved by that, but the gusts that kept slamming into her felt like they were needles of ice that were slicing into every pore.

Then her good palm came down on the cool sensation of her bathroom's tile floor. She never thought cool would feel so good with the whipping cold around her, but it did. She found herself giving into it completely, lunging forward so that her forehead rested against it. Then she was pulling the rest of her body into the small room, and once she'd crossed the threshold, twisted herself around so that she could slam the door closed.

The wind was gone. It may have been swirling through the rest of her apartment, but for a brief moment, with the door closed, she was at peace. She could breathe. The burns or chills that had been on her skin were fading as she lay there on the cool tile floor.

She couldn't stay there forever, though. She knew that. As cool as the tile was on her skin, her palm was still on fire, so she needed to search her drawers for a bandage. She had aloe in one of them as well. She would need to find it. *Aloe was good for burns, right?* She was pretty sure that's what she used in the past. She had used it for sunburn, so it should work for metal burns.

You should go to the hospital and get it checked out, the little voice whispered to her, and she had to laugh at it. Really, did it not think she knew that? Just how the hell was she going to get there? Teleport? She didn't have a lot of options right then for getting out of her damned apartment.

She leaned against the side of her bathtub and used her elbow rather than her hand to push herself up. First, she moved so that she was on her knees. They were still sore, but they didn't feel like they had needles tearing into the flesh anymore. Once she was steady, she used her other hand to push herself so that she could stand.

She kept her hand close to her chest. She looked at it briefly on her way up and didn't like the look of the blackened flesh that had once been her palm. Would that ever heal? It looked like it was far past the point of being saved. The skin was hard and crusted like a charbroiled steak that someone had forgotten about on the grill.

She found herself limping the little distance to her bathroom counter and leaned against it, thankful for its sturdiness. When she needed, Amanda used her left hand to steady herself. She did feel a little woozy but tried to ignore it as she worked to find where she kept what she was looking for.

Thankfully, it didn't take her long, and she had the aloe coated over her palm. It felt cool as she applied it, but she still had to grit her teeth from the pain. Once she had a good layer of it, she tried to finagle the bandage, and the plastic protection wrap one handed. It was a struggle, but on the third bandage, she was finally able to free one without the sticky portions getting caught upon itself and get the Band-Aid so that it was covering her blackened skin.

It wasn't much. It hurt, the sensation of the bandage covering the damaged skin, but she didn't know what else to do.

Just what was she supposed to do? She was locked in the one room in her studio that there was no escape from. It had no windows; it had only the one door. She had the bathroom counter littered with all her normal daily necessities; she had her toilet, and she had her shower. If there was a tornado and she couldn't make it to the basement storm shelter, she could hide there, but other than that, there wasn't much she could do with her bathtub. That wasn't going to do much to keep demons away from her.

She looked at her reflection in the mirror, surprised to see the woman who was staring back at her. She didn't recognize the terrified woman with tear-streaked cheeks who was there. She had always thought of herself as a fighter, but she didn't see that person anymore. Where had that person gone? Had she ever really been there or was that a lie she had told herself?

You know that's a lie. You know you're no fighter. Lexi was the fighter. She was the superhero. At best, you were her sidekick, but even that was a stretch. You were her tech support or eye in the sky. You were never one to fight your battles; you had Lexi to do that. That was until she had her girlfriend and left you all alone for those few months.

Amanda tried not to remember when she'd been relinquished to being the third wheel and didn't have time to debate who she was when the face returned. She had only briefly glimpsed it, looking at her through the mirror, before it pushed through. Its claws she recognized from the one that had held her hand on the door, and now they were pushing her. She didn't have a chance to even catch her breath or scream as she felt herself propelled back, then she was tripping over the edge of her bathtub. She continued to fall. She had lost all control of staying on her feet as they were taken out from under her. She was going down as they were flying up.

Her shower curtain was grabbing at her, tugging at her as she was in the midst of it, but it was going back with her. It wrapped itself around her, the rings that held it in place snapping from the rod above as the pinging sound of broken metal echoed in the small room.

Her back slammed against the far wall, and her ass hit hard against the back ledge, then she went down the rest of the way.

She wrestled the white plastic curtain, frantic to get out of its constraints. She was able to free her head, then looked into the mirror to see if the demon man was coming after her, but he was gone. The room was empty.

She struggled to pull part of the curtain further down, but it wrapped itself tighter around her slender frame. The damn thing was fighting her. She'd thought it was just getting caught with her as she fell, but it grabbed her and pulled itself taut. She fought harder, pushing to get it unwrapped and break away from it, but it slithered from her grasp anytime she tried to get a firm grip.

She looked at the plastic that she was wrapped up in. The curtain she had bought for herself just after moving into the apartment and realizing that places you rented didn't always come with shower curtains. It was one of her first purchases once she had moved in, because even though she lived alone, she didn't like the idea of not having that little bit of privacy that came with having one.

She watched that piece of plastic, a symbol of her first purchase of freedom, slither across her skin like it was a swarm of snakes. She saw different shapes within the plastic, all of them moving, gripping, throbbing as they surrounded her and contracted.

It was getting harder to breathe. Her chest felt like it was beginning to collapse.

The lights flickered and then went out. She was again alone in the black of nothing, though now she could still feel those slithering shapes trying to squeeze the life out of her.

Something else in the darkness growled, a low, rumbling roar. It took her a moment to identify, but she caught on when she saw the green light that worked its way from the gap of her toilet seat and the porcelain. From that little space, a luminescence slowly came to life, and as she watched, a dark shape moved.

The shape growled again and confirmed it was definitely coming from there, but it was answered by another low growl. This one was much closer, and she turned to see that there was more of that unnatural green light coming from her bathtub drain.

However, the light from her drain was quickly blotted out as black ooze came up from below. From that ooze, she watched in horror as it took shape; a large, black creature that loosely resembled a snake.

There was a shudder from her toilet and she looked in time to see a larger creature, much like the one emerging from her drain, had risen from the bowl. It was long like a snake, but as she watched, she could see the large, black eyes that were watching her. Then she watched as the mouth, or what would have been a mouth, split into four distinct heads, each opening to reveal long rows of teeth. The teeth were short, but they looked sharp, and ready to tear into her flesh.

It launched itself at her, landing on her chest. She felt its weight push her back against the wall. The thing was a solid mass that felt like a brick had landed on her as it shifted, turning its head toward her legs. It was fighting to get itself out of the shower curtain. She watched as it tore at the plastic, not having the patience to work its way through the folds. It ripped and fought to shred its way to her inner self.

"No!" she cried out and twisted, struggling with the curtain that had a mind of its own, using her own legs to try to push away the creature. She must have caught it off guard as it was flung free, off her and toward the smaller one that had stayed where it had initially emerged from the drain.

Something shifted around her, and she felt the curtain loosening. She was able to pull herself free as the two snake-like creatures were snapping at each other. She ignored them as best she could, focusing on getting herself up and out of the damned plastic.

If she did get out of this, she would never buy a plastic shower curtain ever again. Maybe next time she'd get cloth. Either that or she was doing baths for life. Fuck this.

She landed on her tile floor after struggling out of the bathtub, but didn't let it slow her momentum, taking the plastic curtain and throwing it back at the creatures that had noticed she was getting away.

She saw them tearing at it as it landed over them, and she didn't pause. She quickly made a dash for her door, not caring if the wind was still tearing apart her apartment.

She opened it and stepped out...

Her apartment was gone. She didn't see it until it was too late, but she had stepped into nothing. What she had expected to be her carpet was instead a dark abyss. One that she had no clue where or what she was falling into. She was lost into nothingness.

CHAPTER 19

Lexi immediately recognized the room she had emerged into and felt like she had somehow transported herself into a work of fiction. Of course she would. This was just how Jacob Skulz had described it in his book, one she had read multiple times. She had transported herself, though instead of finding herself in some fanciful wonderland, she was in a demented hellscape full of demons, sacrifices and decapitations.

The pentagram inside a circle was still where he had written it, free of any kind of debris in the center of the room, which was actually odd. As she recalled, the reason the demon was able to kill Denise, the main character, had been because a piece of furniture crashed down and snapped the copper tubing comprising the outer ring. Once the circle's integrity was broken, the demon had been able to escape and tear her apart. Which, of course, freed him upon the world to wreak havoc.

God, she loved his end of the world endings. They were always so dark and brutal. Why did he have to turn into such an evil psychopath, kidnapping people for his stories?

Her stomach rumbled again, and she was quickly brought back from her adulation of the sick mind of the writer to be reminded she was currently in one of his stories, and right now the only damned thing she really wanted was something to eat. Though if she could find something to use to get out of there, that would also be helpful.

She took stock of the room, pushing away her fan girl thoughts and bringing herself back to her reality. It was a room that appeared like it could have been Skulz's office or library, though it had been modified for the story of Witchy Woman. On one side of the room, the wall was composed of nothing but bookshelves filled to the brim with books. They all appeared to be of various ages and stages of disrepair, some of them rather archaic in their writings.

She was also pretty sure that if she went to the center most bookcase and found the right book, a door would open. It was the only door to the room, and it was hidden on the bookshelf.

Would the door be locked? Skulz had to know the tunnel lead there. This was probably all his plan. He was trying to get her to do things so that it fueled his story. He had to want her there for a reason.

She would check on the door soon. She had to keep checking the room. It wasn't going to do her any good just to rush into another one of his traps.

She looked at the desk to her left. It was a large, ornate desk made of dark cherry wood. It almost looked like a black desk stained in blood as it shined there, almost gleaming from the little desk light that was lit upon it.

Why had the light been on? Why was the overhead light on as well? He didn't just leave all the lights on in his home, so he had to have been in this room recently.

Sure he had. He had got it ready for her once she escaped from the tunnel. It was just more of his mind fucking games. He was watching her; he had to be.

She went past the desk, running her finger along the smooth surface. It was warm to the touch, almost hot, and she felt the heat radiate from it as she walked past. Was it throbbing? She could have sworn that it pulsed as she touched it, like a heartbeat.

She recoiled, backing away from it, and looked at the only other point of interest: the summoning circle. Just as it had been described initially, it was a large circle on the floor, made from a ring carved in the cement, then copper poured to amplify its protection strength. Inside the circle was the pentagram, and for every point that touched the circle, traces of melted wax were the remnants of past summonings.

There wasn't anything else in the room. She could go through the desk, but she doubted she'd find anything in the drawers and that was if the monster of a desk was even unlocked, which was unlikely.

You should still look. Don't discount anything.

The voice was right. Though as she neared it, her skin crawled with the sensation that everything was wrong. A dread washed over her, an uneasiness she just couldn't shake.

She thought about how warm it had been when she'd first walked by it, and wondered why? It wasn't alive. A desk couldn't be alive.

Though as she neared it and thought about how she had felt it throbbing beneath her finger before, she wasn't so sure.

Come on, you're being silly, she thought to herself as she reached it, moving behind to look at the drawers. The handles on each side were decorated with black marble skulls, and she didn't see a place in the wood for a key to be entered. Could the desk be unlocked?

She reached for the first drawer and was surprised when it opened easily in her grasp.

She chuckled at herself for being so silly as she looked at the contents. It was just a regular desk drawer, *and Skulzy, man. You are a slob.* The drawer was cluttered with pencils, pens, and some kind of ruler that looked too small to be really used for anything. There were batteries and even a charging cord for a phone. It was a regular desk drawer. She was shocked by how innate it was. Hell, if she was a writer, it would probably look the same way.

She was getting ready to dig through more drawers when a glint of something shiny caught her attention under a scrap of paper. She shuffled the scrap, and her mouth moistened when she saw the flask.

It was probably alcohol, but that didn't matter. It was liquid or should contain liquid. Right then, it didn't matter. She was thirsty; she was hungry, and that flask was the answer to at least one of the two.

She grabbed it and shook, enjoying the sound of the swooshing contents within.

Cha-ching!

She twisted the cap and didn't hesitate to smell the contents, quickly knocking it back and letting the lukewarm liquid flood into her lips.

What the hell? Who puts water in a flask? She was both amazed, frustrated, and relieved at the taste of the plain tap water as it flowed down her esophagus. It was refreshing, though it was also too much. Her throat wasn't ready for it, being too dry from who knew how long of nothing. She choked, coughing on the water she now struggled to swallow.

Lexi tried not to be too loud, but she was choking. It was getting into her lungs. She couldn't breathe. She could feel the moisture swirling around inside her and she felt like she was suddenly drowning. That her lungs were betraying her as they were filled with fluid.

She leaned forward, dropping the flask as she put both hands on the desk, going into a fit of uncontrollable coughing.

She hadn't had that much; the water shouldn't be filling her like this.

The coughing spasm continued. Her lungs burned as they tried to expel it. Her throat became raw, and she could taste the traces of bile and blood.

It took her a moment, but she could feel the tickle in her lungs that was forcing her to struggle to exhume the liquid from her. She began breathing in short gasps, still feeling the little bit of moisture inside her.

Her head was swirling as she concentrated on breathing regularly. She coughed one more time, this one under her own control, and was just trying to get more of that annoying liquid out from where it was not supposed to be. Then she was taking large mouthfuls of air.

After a few moments, everything was calm again, and she licked her lips, feeling that intense thirst come back. She looked back at the flask, now cautious, but still tempted. Her throat was on fire. She wanted something cool and refreshing even more.

It was just water. Drink it slow and don't be a dumbass this time. She took another drink. This time she went slowly, sipping the water and embracing it, feeling it work its way down her throat.

It felt good. It was warm, but she could still feel each droplet as it raced down into her stomach. She kept sipping at it, and before she realized it, the last drop fell into her open mouth. It was gone, but it had helped so much.

Her stomach grumbled, its voice loud in the room even to her ears. Did stomachs have voices? It growled like it was its own beast, ready to rampage now that she had water. Now it wanted its own due.

Thankfully, as she set back the flask, she eyed the protein bar that had been buried next to it.

Well, that made sense, right? If this had been where Skulz had at one time written one of his books, why not have a snack and water there for those moments when he needed it?

157

She didn't know how old it was and didn't care. She ripped away that wrapper and worked to devour it. It tasted like old, stale cardboard, and she loved every bite of it.

When she was done, she felt satisfied. She wasn't full, though with how her stomach still continued to make noises, she might have thought she was. The protein bar twisted inside of her gut, and it gurgled in response.

At least her head began clearing. It wasn't much; the food wasn't even being digested yet, but the mere presence of it in her body gave her a boost of energy and a sense of recognition of her current state.

She looked down at her blood-soaked shirt, that had been ripped in multiple places. One of her breasts was exposed, and she had been oblivious to it. She could see where the bone had stabbed her just beneath it, and the dried blood that coated her stomach. There were multiple other scrapes scattered across her pale skin.

Then there were her shorts. They were stained brown and yellow; her having shit and pissed herself in her time trapped down there.

She was a fucking mess. A disgusting mess, and just what the hell was she going to do now?

Continue looking through the desk. Maybe there will be a weapon or something. You just need to take control of the story. Take it from him.

But who was controlling the story? What did she need to do? Did she need to kill him? Was it just that she needed to escape? If she escaped, who was to say he wouldn't bring her back? If she killed him, would that truly be the end? What about that thing she had seen back there?

Lexi opened the next drawer and quickly closed it. Just a ream of paper. A ream of paper for which he must have planned to use to write his next book. It didn't help her, but maybe the next drawer...

Lexi gasped when she saw the pair of eyes looking up at her. She recognized those dark brown eyes, black hair, and darkened skin. It matched the description perfectly for Denise. She had brought the demon into this world and had set it free. It had killed her and taken her head as its prize before it had escaped to wreak its havoc.

She was well preserved. The book had described her as a witch. Could she have had some kind of power? How had Jacob trapped her there? How had he tricked her?

And if she truly had been a witch, then why did she know very little about witchcraft? In the book, she'd been left in this room and had studied all the books until she'd learned what she'd thought was enough to control the demon.

Did anyone ever know enough about such an impossible task? Lexi didn't think they did. It became only a matter of desperation and how far one was willing to go to survive.

Lexi looked at those lifeless eyes and wondered just how she had been lured into Jacob's trap? Probably how he got most of his victims, with some form of bait. He must have had something to get her there and then once he did, the trap was sprung. Then she was his to watch.

From his books, she could see how Jacob never did any of his own killing. He set the stage, but the world around him always did the work. He was just a voyeur, a watcher.

So, what was going to kill her? The demon? Was that what had been in the room with her? It made sense. If Jacob was still working with it, would he really use the same plot device?

That had probably not been his original intention, but when she didn't fall into what he had really wanted, he was probably trying to make something work.

Lexi grimaced. Bad novels always came from when writers tried to force an idea that wasn't working. She could think of one or two of his that had felt forced. Now that he was no longer on a pedestal, she felt like she could see more holes in his work.

So, what are you going to do to stop him? This was her story. She needed to stop him, not the story, but him.

She looked at the head and then the circle before looking at the books on the wall. All those books, so many of them dealing with witchcraft and demonology. She knew what the Witchy Woman had done wrong, so in theory she could keep from making the same mistake.

She just needed the one thing that would make it work. She needed to remember its name. Had the name Jacob used in the book been correct? She had no way of knowing, not that she remembered it. Max was the shortened christening of it, but it had only been mentioned once in the whole book. She remembered because when she read it, it had hurt her eyes, and she'd had a migraine the rest of the night.

What had been that name? There was so much power in names. Reading books had taught her that. That is, if any of it was true. There was so much power in a name, and with hellbound creatures, there was a level of control. She just needed to remember...

MISSING PERSONS: LEXI PEABODY
VIDEO EXCERPT

Hey Flix fam! LexiSexyReads here again for another video and sorry, fam, but I don't have a book recommendation. Why? Because my girlfriend had the bright idea that we should go camping.

Now I get that there are people out there that like to be cut off in the world, no cell service, no internet, no electricity, but I'm not one of these people. Like seriously, what was she thinking? I mean, do I look like I want to be in a tent for a weekend? Did I ever give off the impression that I like to hike?

If so, you have got the wrong gal, and you don't know me. I read way too many horror books about what happens out there to ever want any of that.

Okay. So, I guess I'll give one recommendation. Bishop, great novel, about a werewolf or werebear... something like that.

I mean, I could be out in the woods and become something's lunch. And you wouldn't want that. I wouldn't want that.

And to top it all off, there was no place to shower or bath. I had to do the whole weekend stinkified because it was hot. I was sweaty and there was nothing I could do about it. It was horrible. Why do people do that to themselves?

All I have to say is that when I got home, I was ready to sell my soul for a warm bath. My muscles hurt, my skin felt crusty and nasty. It hurt as well. Everywhere hurt.

I soaked in my bathtub and then I took a shower again after that. I still don't feel clean.

But I'm back now. Rant over. I'll be getting back on the book recommendations later today.

Be good everyone and remember LexiSexyReads here telling you to stay sexy and read more books.

CHAPTER 20

"You have been such a fun plaything. Come on, little toy, time to wake up. There's someone here that wants to meet you."

"Just how rough were you with her?"

"Oh, you'll see. I'll show it all to you. I'll give you all her pain."

"Yeah, whatever, just as long as it's going to make a good story."

"I don't know about that, but I had fun."

Amanda heard the voices but had a hard time catching the words. Where was she? She remembered falling. She had been falling in darkness for so long that she wasn't sure when she had drifted off to sleep. She hadn't thought that would even have been possible, but she had been falling and screaming. Eventually, she lost her voice and shortly after, consciousness.

And now this? But what was this?

Amanda tried to open her eyes and was met with searing pain that shot across her forehead, her temples stabbing her with resistance to the brightness.

There was a flash of light, then she could feel herself lying on a hard, cold floor. She was blinking her eyes, that intense pain fading as she was finally able to flutter them open. Now, if only the aching pain in the rest of her head and body would go away. Her joints hurt and her teeth felt like she'd been grinding them all night.

When she could get her eyes to stay open, she tried to focus on her surroundings, but it was dark, and sensations tickled her face. It was like something light was attempting to get her to sneeze by sticking a feather near her nose.

She moved slowly and felt the gentle tug of her own hair. She reached out to pull her long auburn hair back from over her face and started to push herself up. She must be on her tile floor. She had fallen asleep and had drifted off.

She had been thinking about that writer and had remembered some of his books. She had drifted off and fallen asleep in her bathroom. There was a lot going on this week, and she had been exhausted. It had all just caught up to her. She was fine. She was in her bathroom.

Her bathroom floor wasn't cement.

She looked at the rough surface beneath her hand. It was rough and grey. It looked like the laundry room in the basement of her apartment complex. How would she have ever gotten there?

She pulled her hair back further, tossing it over her shoulder. Sometimes she really hated having all that damn hair.

Her breath caught in her throat as she looked around her. She was not in the basement. She didn't know where she was. It was an oddly shaped room, but she had trouble taking in the weird walls and what looked like a shelf in the back.

She was surrounded by bones. Human bones, she was sure of it. There was a part of a body...

Holy fuck, there was part of a naked woman, her torso and half her face, just lying in the corner, turned so that it looked like she was watching her. *What the fuck? What the ever-loving fuck. Where was she?* There was a dead body. Sure, there were bones all over the place, but there was a part of a dead body, and that dead eye looking right at her.

"Fuck, fuck, fuck, fuck, FUCK!" she hissed as she quickly started back-peddling on the floor but was thwarted when her hand came down on something sharp biting into her palm. The burned flash and sharp stabbing made her remember the demon and its clawed hand.

Amanda crashed back, her butt landing on the cement, but she kept scooching away. There was no thought in it. She just needed to get away from that dead eye. She didn't notice that there were more bones around her, closer to her, and that she was starting to push herself through them. She didn't know where she was going. She was quickly looking around, trying to take in more of the room.

There were more of the skeletons in different states of decay, but she stopped when she saw the man standing in front of a large metal door. She wasn't sure, but she thought she recognized him but couldn't place him.

He stood there watching her with his large glasses, and she noticed he was a little taller than her with silver hair and a goatee. The damn asshole was watching her freaking out, hadn't said a word, but just smirked at her.

He must be the writer, though for right now the bastard's name escaped her.

She looked around the room again. This man had Lexi. Had he brought her there? Was there any trace of her? Amanda didn't see any, but she noticed the large puddle of what she assumed was dried blood near the half ripped apart torso. The more she looked at the body, she realized it was not as fresh as she had first believed, but Amanda felt like that blood was much more recent. Was it Lexi's? Was she already dead?

Fuck, what did she get her stupid ass into? What the fuck had she been thinking? How could she have been so dumb?

"I told you she was a fun plaything," a raspy, gravelly voice spoke, and she felt the hot breath on her neck.

Amanda spun around, but there was no one there. The writer was still standing by the door.

"Well, isn't this interesting? I've never had someone give me their address before, knowing what I do. That does make you an interesting character. Though, of course, you thought you were going to have the FBI catch me or what, your detective friend? Maybe even... your friend's mother? What had you called her, Tee? Yes, that was it."

Amanda's jaw nearly hit the floor. Just how in the hell did he know so much? She tried to recover, but her mind was reeling.

"Where's Lexi?"

"Oh, is that your friend's name?"

"Don't give me that. You knew Tee. You sure as hell know Lexi's name."

"We'll see. That's her RL name. I don't care so much about that. See, she's already a character in the story, so she's already lost that name. I almost completely forgot it. Now Tee, that's just such a great nickname, and so random and simple. I'm not going to do anything with that. She can keep it."

"Don't give me that bullshit. Where is she?"

The writer shrugged and looked at her like he truly didn't care to ever answer her, so she was surprised when he did.

"I don't know. That's the funny thing with haunted houses and demons on the loose. They do all sorts of things on their own. I only find out later when they share it with me. This place makes for such wonderful dreams, though I'm sure many of them would call them nightmares. It would be enough to drive someone insane. At least it did for the previous owners. Me, not so much. I love having dreams of houses crushing people or electrifying them. This house really is temperamental. I'd try to stay on her good side if I were you."

"You're lying! Where is Lexi?!"

"I really don't know." The writer was laughing now, fully amused, as she looked desperately around the room. "I left her right there-" he said, pointing to the spot on the floor. "She looked pretty dead to me; she'd bled out. I was fully looking forward to getting you in here and having you see her lying there. Color me surprised and a little disappointed that her body was gone. Thank you, you fucking house. Great way for a fucking plot twist."

Amanda took advantage of the fact that the writer had stopped watching her and had started screaming at the house. She wasn't a physical person, but the moment his eyes were off her, she leaped forward and reached out, slicing with her hands. She didn't have that much for nails, the last week having her becoming an obsessive nail biter, but she slashed down with what she had.

He turned just as she was getting close, but it was too late. She brought down one hand as though it was a claw, tearing away at his cheek, then she brought down the other one and did the same on the other side.

She was frustrated that she didn't feel like she had done much, but she didn't stop to analyze the damage. Her momentum propelled her forward, and she slammed into him. Her arms flailed, not so much coordinating an attack but continuing to slash with what she had wherever she saw exposed flesh. She tried to get to his eye, but he was fast enough to get his hands up to keep her from making purchase. However, the harder he tried to protect his eyes, the more of his face it left for her to keep tearing at.

She felt it when they crashed into the door behind him, and she heard the air rush from his lungs.

Good, let the bastard know how it is to struggle to scream.

She kept clawing. She wasn't going to stop. If she didn't have her friend, she sure as hell wanted to make the writer pay for it.

"Ma-" the writer started to say, but she brought her hand down and scraped it along his lips. It turned into more of a slap, but it took the words in his mouth and kept them there.

The writer struggled to worm his way out from under her. He was both bigger and taller than her, and as he was able to get his weight under him, Amanda could feel the shift as he was pushing her to the side. Her own fight was working against her as she had been continuing to push her own mass against him, as little of it as there was, and now the shift meant she was just moving herself faster to the door. She tried to stop, but it was too late. As he finished slipping out from under her assault, she slammed into the door and in one quick motion, he grabbed both her arms.

He had her.

"Fuck face!" she screamed and started kicking him. She was barefoot, *where the fuck had my shoes gone*, but she put as much strength as she could to get him in his shins. She kept kicking. He had her arms; it gave her the chance to use what weight she could as he held her up.

"Fuck! Max! A little help here?" the writer finally spat out as he struggled to withstand her barrage.

Somewhere in the depths of the small room, a low chuckle rumbled from nothing.

"No," the deep, gravelly voice said. She still couldn't see the source, but it sounded like it came from across the room. Its voice, the rumble of boulders shattering, sent a shiver down her spine.

It had unnerved her, but it had completely shaken the writer. He had turned in the direction of the voice and she could see his shock at being defied.

"What do you me-" He didn't get a chance to finish what he was saying because, when his attention faltered, Amanda threw her weight at him again. This time he was completely caught off guard and, with the door no longer behind him, they found themselves falling. He had lost his balance and still had her arms in his grasp, bringing her down with him. She made sure she shifted her weight to land as hard as she could on top of him.

She felt the air escape out of him, and he writhed under her, struggling to pull in a breath. His mouth was opening and closing, his eyes bulging, reminding her of a fish out of water, as he fought his own lungs and the girl on top of him. He was twisting, trying to get her off, but she braced her legs, locking them to the cement floor so that she could put as much of her weight as possible on him.

As much as she wanted to believe she was killing the bastard, she could feel him starting to take deeper breaths, the rising of his chest pushing against her as she fought to keep him down.

"Max... Help..." the writer gasped, still struggling to get air and to get her off of him. He was twisting with more force now, but still had her arms. It was almost as much a hindrance, but he tried to keep hold. Which was probably smart, because she wanted to rip his fucking eyes out.

"No," that voice rumbled again. Amanda noticed that it had not moved closer to them, and she felt like it was watching.

"You... are... bound to... me. Help."

Amanda looked at the writhing shape below her and at where she'd heard that voice. She still didn't see anything there, but she could feel it. She was sure of it now.

"But if you die, I'm free. You should know better than to put yourself in harm's way. I told you she is fun."

Amanda felt her breath catch in her throat, momentarily remembering being trapped in her bathtub as some snake-like creature prepared to strike her.

That was a mistake, as she lost focus. Her legs unlocked, and that was all he needed. She felt herself shoved to the side and then she was rolling into the bones scattered on the floor.

"Oh, yes, she is so much fun. I think maybe I will play with her."

"No!" the writer said. He had been quick to get to his feet and now was backing to the door, already reaching to pull it open. "You'll get your time. Let her simmer in here first."

"But I want to play," the voice spat out the words. She could feel it much closer now, close enough that she thought she could smell it. It was intense; the putrid odor of wet dog and rotten meat swirling around with a hint of cinnamon. She had to stifle the gag that was working its way up.

"Max, down. You should have thought of that when I needed you."

"I'm not some pet to be commanded." She could feel the breath now; the heat from every word stinging her neck.

"Max! Don't make me do it. I said down."

Amanda didn't hear a reply, but she could feel the rhythmic exhale as it hovered behind her. With what sounded like a growl, she felt it back away.

"Good," the writer said as he opened the door. She couldn't see past the darkness of the threshold, but tried to estimate what it would take to get past him. She stopped when she realized he had turned his attention on her.

"I think you're going to have a lot of fun with your new buddy here. Max really seems to like you. He has a lot of fun with the ones he likes."

"Fuck you! Where's Lexi?"

"I'd stop worrying about her. After all, you're the main character now, Sydney. Looks like she was just the Drew Barrymore. You better make yourself comfortable." The writer started to close the door behind him, but then he came back. He fixed his glasses and looked at her. It looked like he wanted to say something, but each time, words were forgotten.

"This will be the last room you ever see, you bitch. Nobody ever attacks me. I'm the writer. I'm not the story. I'm not here. You don't get to do that, understand?" he finally seethed. Then he slammed the door shut. She heard the sound of heavy locks, and then nothing. The room fell into utter silence.

She looked around, watching to see if anything moved. Was the thing still there, or had it listened to the writer? She tried to steady her breathing so she could listen, unsure if she was alone.

Time dragged on; she didn't know for how long. She was just about to accept the fact that she was all alone...

Then there was a gravelly harrumph and a long sigh, the heat from which was directly on her neck.

CHAPTER 21

Lexi worked her way through the books on the shelves, looking at each one and trying to judge if any of them would have the information that she wanted. There was a demon. Jacob's name for it was Max, and somewhere in this collection had to be the answer as to how to control it. At least, that was what she was hoping.

So far, she hadn't seen anything that looked like it was even the slightest bit of use. Though she also knew she had no clue what she was looking for, just that she needed to find it. Lexi knew she did not have much time. Who knew how long it would be before Jacob realized she was missing and would be looking for her? She had to be careful.

Her stomach gurgled and then felt it like something dropped inside her. She physically felt the shift and then the pressure as suddenly her lower intestines, her sphincter, were all working in unison, telling her she didn't have long.

She grabbed the bookshelf, locked her legs and pushed herself onto her tiptoes, counting down the seconds until the sensation passed.

Breathe. Just breathe.

She needed to find a bathroom, though laughed at how absurd that was. She was already covered in her own piss and shit, but sure, let's just risk your life so you can have the luxury now to shit on a toilet.

Moisture touched at the edge of her eyes, and she wanted to scream. Yes, she was ready to put her life on the line, because she was done being the victim. She was done doing this to herself.

The sensation faded, and she gingerly lowered herself, stopping from pushing so hard on the wall.

She released her jaw, not realizing she had clenched it as well. Not sure if it was from the pressure or to keep herself from yelling.

Find the lock. She needed to get out of there. She was not about to soil herself again. From reading Witchy Woman, she had an idea of where the locking mechanism was. She found it and was relieved when she heard the click.

On the wall of bookshelves, one of the sections popped forward an inch. She slowly pulled it open the rest of the way, holding her breath as she listened. The shelf moved easily and, to her relief, quietly.

She peeked through the opening, holding her breath to take in what she saw.

It was beautiful, in a dark, gothic, Halloween-is-everyday sort of way. She saw a long hallway that had ornate pillars that stood floor to ceiling every few feet. They matched the walls and the desk behind her in that dark cherry red-black swirling color that was both creepy and breathtaking at the same time. It was all wood, carved and looked thick. This house must have been old, as every part of it looked handcrafted, with carvings on nearly every surface. To match it, the hallway was lit by what looked like actual candle lit sconces that were nestled between each pillar.

It was a whole vibe that Lexi had to push down the excitement in taking it all in. She hadn't known houses were built like this in the US. It was something like out of what she imagined for gothic European castles.

Something she'd always wanted to travel overseas to see but had never been able to afford to do so.

There was even... she thought she was imagining at first, but as she took in the surroundings, there was quiet music that flowed down the hall. It was soothing, simple music, as though a harp was being played somewhere in the distance.

She would have stood there in awestruck fascination longer, but the pressure returned, and she had to clench again to keep from defecating all over the floor.

She worked on her breathing, keeping an eye on the hallway for any movement while she tried to Frankenstein walk. She was using the wall, pressing on it, partially leaning as she did.

The wall's carvings were smooth and curved beneath her hands and it felt warm to the touch, much like the desk, throbbing like a heartbeat in that same pitter-patter of a rhythm.

She was thankful when the pressure passed, but it didn't fade as much as before. There was still slight pressure that told her if she didn't find a bathroom soon, she wasn't going to make it in time.

What if Jacob was in there? What if he came out of these rooms? She kept an eye out, always sure that he was going to show up at any time, ready to lock her back in the bone room.

She made her way to the first door and stopped when she reached for the doorknob in the shape of a silver skull, the empty sockets looking in her direction. She grabbed it and twisted, glad when it turned. She could feel the pressure coming back.

Easing the door open, she was thrown off by the room. It was a small bathroom, not a full one, but it had a black toilet and a black sink, with no mirror. The floor was red tile, and the walls had more of that carved cherry wood, but in there, there were carvings of faces, each looking as

175

though they were caught while screaming. Every face, all of them at her own height, was looking at her and they were locked in a state of horror.

She nervously took a step into the room, relieved that the light was not by candle, but by a row of led lights that were wrapped around the back of a mount for a mirror, but in its place was a painting. In contrast to the old school gothic hallway behind her, the bathroom was like modern gothic. Either that or it was some reject from a nineties yuppy. She wasn't sure, but she liked it more than she wanted to admit to herself.

She eased the rest of the way into the room, again clamping against the pressure. She leaned on the sink, reached out, and gingerly closed the door behind her. She didn't like the idea of making herself vulnerable and couldn't think of a more vulnerable situation than sitting on the toilet.

She continued to hear that harp playing, and her nervousness about being in the bathroom, of making herself uncomfortable, faded. She heard those strummed chords and found herself giving into it, letting it relax her fears.

She'd lock the door. That heavy door, no one was getting through it. She would be safe in there.

That is, if the door had a lock. As the pressure again eased, she looked at the door and couldn't find one.

Damn.

Damn, damn.

She had no choice. After all, it was all going to be okay. The music told her so.

* * * *

Once she had finished, she felt more human than she thought was possible. What had she been becoming? She wasn't sure, but the thought of putting back on the shorts

176

and shirt she had been wearing was sickening. She could see the stains now, the defecation, the ripped fabric, and they were all reminders of what she had survived.

It's not over yet.

No, it wasn't, but for right then, she was human, and putting those clothes back on, it just didn't feel like the way she was going to survive.

What she really wanted was to clean herself. She didn't want to go back to becoming that animal that had been moving around in those garments. She wanted to become human. She wanted to live, and she needed to feel that.

So, what are you going to do?

She wasn't sure. What was her other option? To go naked?

The house wasn't warm enough for that, even if she felt comfortable doing it.

She shivered as she worked back into her shorts, though at this point, they barely stayed up as it was. How much weight had she lost? This was never the way she had wanted to lose those few pounds, but her clothes had grown slack. Now that they weren't stuck to her, they were threatening to slip off on their own. She didn't even bother with her panties; those were disgusting beyond gag inducing and she would never have them touch her skin again.

Her shirt was another problem. As it turned out, it had been ripped more than she realized. Maybe it had been torn more when she had pulled it off, as now when she tried to put it on, the shirt was little more than tattered cloth, not able to stay covering her chest.

She didn't like being topless, but it wasn't working.

Now, if only she could find some kind of weapon. She looked around the room, but there wasn't anything. There wasn't even a mirror that she could break. No, the only thing she had was toilet paper.

Death by toilet paper. Yeah, that wasn't a thing. Not unless she could get him on the ground and stuff wads and wads of it down his throat. Which, now that she was thinking about it, was not that bad of a visual. The thought of ramming shit coated toilet paper down his throat while he struggled to breathe was a thought that would keep her going.

She needed to keep exploring. There had to be more to this house. It looked big, so she would keep looking until she found something.

She opened the door, ready to go back into the hallway and explore. She stopped when she saw there was no hallway on the other side.

"What the fuck?"

CHAPTER 22

Lexi took in what had replaced the hallway. It didn't make sense. It had been the same door she'd come through, but yet it wasn't. How was that possible? Rooms don't change. Doors don't lead to other destinations. She had come into the bathroom. There was one door. She went to go out that door. She should be back in the hallway, but instead, she wasn't sure what you would call the room- a bathtub room? Does that even exist?

The room was large, so much so that she couldn't see the back wall as it was lost to darkness, and there wasn't anything in the room except a large, black, freestanding, clawfoot bathtub. Lexi had never seen anything like it outside of pictures. It was beautiful, filled with a steaming hot bubble bath. How, she didn't know, as she could not see any water or drainage lines connected to it.

The room only featured one other item. A fireplace with a crackling fire. The light reached out from it, but did not make it any further than the bathtub, making it hard to see the walls.

What else was there that she could not see? This was obviously a trap for her, but the tub looked so inviting. And where else did she have to go?

There you go, putting yourself in another compromising position. That voice nagged at her from the back of her mind.

Yet, as the voice screamed at her about putting herself in such an exposed way, that music, the beautiful chords being strummed told her it would be okay. Everything was fine. She was safe. She just needed to get herself clean, and it would all be okay.

She tried to zone out the music. If she went in there, she'd be naked, and it would be hard to attack if something came after her.

What would attack? With so large an area around her, she'd have time to react. Just she'd still need some kind of weapon to fight back with.

So, what else was new?

She looked at the fireplace, caught up in the soothing warmth and the calming smell of burning wood. As much as she hated camping, there was something to be said about a warm fire.

She'd always dreamed of owning a house with a fireplace, somewhere she could cozy up to someone warm and they would just sit there for hours in each other's arms. Then she could do awesome videos in front of it, fireside book reviews or something like that. It would probably get lots of likes. It would really set her videos apart from all the other flixers out there.

She walked over to the fireplace, not ready to be seduced by the warm tub that was trying to lure her into its temptation.

Like the bathroom, the surrounding pillars were carved with a column of faces, all fixed in that state of horror. Some were men, some were woman, all of them screaming. Some looked like they were missing part of their heads, like something had beaten them, some were missing eyes, but all of it was wonderfully carved so there was no mistaking that this was intentional in the craftsmanship. Those faces were all meant to be deformed, and it was a part of the art from which they were displayed.

Before she realized she was doing it, she reached out and ran her hand along the carvings, feeling the brutality of how they died, and running her fingers through it. Her breath caught for a moment when her finger pricked on something sharp, and she quickly pulled her finger to her mouth as it bled. It was only a drop, but she studied where the sharp piece of a skull had cut her. It was obvious a large chunk had been taken out of the person, probably from something heavy smashing down on him.

She looked around the room, checking to make sure she was still alone. She didn't feel uneasy there. In fact, being in the room was the most relaxed she had felt in her entirety of being in the hell house. For the first time, she wasn't afraid for her life.

Of course you're not. The door is gone.

She hadn't paid attention to it so much when she looked around, but now that the nagging voice was pointing it out, she noticed that sure enough, the door was gone. There was now only the fireplace and the tub, the rest were gone into darkness.

That bathtub looked so warm and inviting. She couldn't really take a bath there, could she? Whoever had filled it would be coming back to take their bath.

But she knew they wouldn't. That bath was for her. The music said so. Everything else was unimportant, she just needed to take the bath.

Haven't you ever felt so dirty that your only desire was to be clean? You just need to lower yourself into that alluring water. Cleanse yourself in his blood...

But it wasn't blood, it was water. At least, it looked like water to her.

Not that she would take advantage of it and leave herself without any kind of weapon. How foolish did Jacob think she was?

But Jacob didn't run the bath for her. She didn't know how she knew, but as soon as she thought it, she realized she was right.

So, who, how, why? The questions tried to flood her, but that calming warmth of the fire and the music continued to nudge them away.

What if you had a weapon with you in the bath? You'd feel safe then, right?

Somehow, she knew that no matter what, even with a weapon, she should not be getting in that water. There was no way for it to ever be safe. She couldn't do it...

The music grew louder, invading her thoughts again, soothing her, calming her nerves. It was almost like she could hear a voice in the strumming of the chords, telling her it was going to be okay. Everything was going to be fine; she could get into the water.

She thought about it, and yes, if she had a knife or something, then maybe she would feel safe taking the bath. After all, she could see anyone coming to get her from any direction.

She looked back to the fireplace and noticed there was a stand of tools for its maintenance. They were gold, and the handles were like so much of the house, flourished by a carved skull. There was the ash shovel, who knew if it had any kind of better name, but there was also the poker, with its sharp, reaper-like edge.

She could take that with her. That would keep her safe.

She grabbed it and felt the warmth of it in her hand as it filled her with a sense of security. It felt good in her hand, and she did a few test swings with it. Oh yeah, she could do some damage with that bad boy. Hell, looking at the face where she had cut herself, it looked just about right to cause that kind of damage. She could bash Jacob's skull in if she got him right.

She had a weapon.

But what if the other thing came for her? What about Max?

She would deal with that when the time came. For now, she was armed, and she had a bath. Who could fault her for wanting to get some of the crap that had dried to her body off?

She undressed and eased herself into the tub, experiencing a shock at just how deep it was. It also felt heavy, like there was no way anything was going to move it. She was able to climb over the edge and slip down, easing herself to lie in the water until it was up to her neck.

She had not realized just how much she missed that little bit of civilization until she was devoured by it.

MISSING PERSONS: LEXI PEABODY
VIDEO EXCERPT

Hey Flix fam! LexiSexyReads back again, and I'm upset. I mean come on!

So, what's happened? I got dumped. Me. She said I was too girlie because I didn't like the outdoors.

I am not one of these girlie girl prom queens. Oh no, but you have the gall to say that you can't be with someone just because she does her nails and would prefer not to be hiking.

First off, you didn't tell me we were hiking until we were out there. I did not have boots for it. I was not ready for it.

You know what I think? Really? I think you were just looking for an excuse. You were not happy, and you were looking for a reason, but instead of talking about it, you had to play this little game.

If you weren't happy, you could have just talked to me. You could have woman'd up and said, 'Lexi, let's talk. I think we should split up.'

Had we talked, that would have been one thing, but you want to play these games?

What's wrong with you? I am a person, one that thought you had feelings for me.

You know what you did? You treated me like dirt, like garbage, something that was beneath you.

185

You knew my family and how they treated me, and how that all made me feel. So, what do you do? You find a way to do something worse.

You broke up with me because I'm too girlie, that I sit on my phone all the time making my silly little videos. Well, you know what? These flixies, you guys out there watching this video, you are my family. It's not that basket case I have at home, or that asshole who wants me to call him dad, stepdad, whatever.

My family is you guys. My flixies. You guys get me, you're here for me and I love you.

And I'm not just some girlie girl. I take my self-defense classes and in a dark alley I know I can kick your ass, so you better watch yourself.

You think my videos are silly, that my followers are silly, well here is the thing. My followers are growing, and they are my family. They are my army. And we will make your life hell.

-User Deleted Video

CHAPTER 23

Lexi must have dozed off as she woke and felt a change in the room. She was no longer alone. She sensed there was another presence moving towards her, though she couldn't see where.

The water felt like it had lost some of its heat and the firelight was waning since the logs had burned down to embers.

Lexi tightened her grip on the poker she held just beneath the water as a chill ran through her.

The water rippled in front of her. Without hesitation, the poker was rising out of the water and slicing through the open air.

A chuckle responded. Its source was unknown, as it sounded like it echoed from all around her. It was that gravelly voice she had heard before.

"Hello, Max," she growled through gritted teeth.

"Why hello, little plaything. Did you enjoy the bath I prepared for you?" the demon said, his voice coming from behind her. She could feel the heat of it on the back of her neck.

She gripped the poker tighter. She had brought it back into the water but left the tip visible.

"You don't need that. I'm not here to hurt you."

Nearby, she heard the dull thud and clatter of wood falling and looked to see that more had been added to the fire. It was quickly catching, the fire hungry for more food to embrace. The warmth from which was already reaching her.

The water was getting warm as well. She knew the fire wasn't doing it, so something else had to be heating it. As far as she knew, there was a fire underneath her and the tub was some pot for her to be cooked alive.

But it never got too warm. It was heated to just how she liked it, which Tina, her ex- girlfriend, had once joked that it was just shy of lava.

Tina. It had been so long since Lexi had thought of her. Every memory was laced now with such vitriol, as all she wanted was to make her suffer. She wanted so many of them to suffer. On camera she always played nice, tried to make everyone think she was polite, but once the camera was off there were so many times, she wanted to tear people apart, rip their eyes out, spit into their freshly emptied eye sockets and use their decapitated heads as bowling balls.

Maybe that was why she always enjoyed Skulz's books so much. They were a release for a lot of that anger that she fought to hold inside her. She was mad at the world and Jacob gave her a place where she could see that anger getting its release.

Though she never wanted to be the one who was getting killed in one of his books. That was just God's twisted version of karma.

"Why don't you just kill me and get it over with?"

"Not yet, puppet. I'm not done playing with my other toy right now, though I think I'll pay her a visit soon. No, I wanted to give you a chance to relax. You've been through so much."

"Why?"

In the few remaining bubbles, she saw a line running through the water. It started at the bottom of the tub but slowly made its way towards her.

"Oh, there are other sins to explore, other ways to play. Do you want to play with me?"

"Ne-" she had been about to curse the thing, yelling she would never play with it, but the word caught in her throat. She stopped herself and instead shifted in the tub, pulling herself to sit a little straighter before responding with, "Maybe, but what do you have in mind?"

"Oh, we can have all kinds of fun."

"Yeah?"

That low growling chuckle again rumbled through the room. "Yeah."

"Why me?"

"You know, you are different than so many of his other victims. Stronger. A fighter. So many of them when faced with death gave in so easily. You would think that when faced with it, they would put all their energy into fighting to stay alive, but so many don't believe that it's finally their time. They think someone is going to come in and save them. Not you. You know there is no savior."

"Tell me your name," she said, trying to ooze as much of her video persona as she could. She'd never been one to really capture her online persona into the everyday, but she was doing her best to channel LexiSexy as much as possible.

The chuckling laughter blossomed into a hearty laugh the caused ripples in the water and it shook the room.

"Silly, silly plaything. Your obsession with names. You try to bind me from the writer? You think it would be that easy. Names have power but not in what you seek. You need not a name but knowledge."

"And what do I do to gain such knowledge?"

"Knowledge isn't gained but earned."

Lexi shifted again, this time crossing her legs in the tub. The tub no longer felt like it had been as big as before and the room started to feel like it was suffocating her, the smoke choking her in her lungs.

What had she been thinking? Was she really trying to seduce a demon? She no longer felt as brazen as she had only moments ago, realizing just how stupid she was being.

Even in the warm water, a chill ran through her as she looked around, trying to see if she could spot where it was, if it was directly over her still or had gone somewhere else in the room.

"I'm still here and it's only me," it said. Again, it was behind her, and she felt its breath on her ear.

"I'm going to die here," Lexi said, feeling the pain in her chest as the certainty was rising up inside her. She had the poker, but what good was that going to do? She couldn't go through with it. She wasn't about to give up her body to this beast, no matter what game it played with her, and she had no way of killing it with just the rod of metal in her hands. The deformed heads in the fireplace were evidence of that. She was sure those were past victims, all thinking they could fight their way free.

"Probably." The demon said, and to her surprise, she heard it as it took a step on the tiled floor. It was behind her, but she could hear as it started to walk around the tub. She looked up, and sure enough, she could see it.

It was all black, nearly invisible to the shadows behind her as the light barely reflected off its scales that were darkness personified, the darkest of shades. There were patches of fur in various spots along its arms and legs, and then there were its hooved feet that echoed with each step. The thing was completely naked, and as such, she saw its enormous member that swayed as it walked. The damn thing was nearly presenting it to her as it was at eye level. He walked, staying turned to her while he came around to the foot of the bathtub.

It knew what it was doing too, as she looked at its face and saw its mouth curled up in a smirk, revealing its fanged teeth as it looked at her. Its red, burning eyes studying her, its large horns protruding from its temples like a bull.

"Then why don't you kill me now? Just be done with it."

"I should. The vessel would like that. He would see what I would show him, and I could tear you apart, feast on your flesh, and enjoy every morsel of your sex. After killing you, I might even have my way with your body in every carnal way, though I guess I could make it more interesting and do it while you were alive first, enjoying your screams as I took you again and again.

"I could do so, just as I had with so many other fleshies. Not everyone who comes here makes it into the pages of his books. There are many that do not make the cut for his next story.

"He feeds me well with so many to torment."

"So why haven't you?"

"I don't know. I was going to. When you first entered his study, I was prepared to rise out of the circle and play with you. I would let you think you were safe, have you beg me to kill him, and then I would break free. It's almost impossible to see, but there is a break in the copper ring. It's enough. I've done it before."

"And you didn't."

"I didn't."

"Why?"

"I don't know."

The demon stood there, eyeing her. It kept her fixed in its gaze, and she noticed the little twitch of its member while it was watching her.

"You're bored." Lexi said.

"Maybe."

"You are. So, what do you want with me?"

"You. Nothing. What could a human give me?"

"You want something."

"Not anything from a human."

"You bonded to Jacob. I could get you free."

"Like so many have offered before. You think you are so special?"

"I don't know. Why haven't you killed me yet?"

The demon lunged forward, its claws grabbing the side of the tub as it loomed over so that its face was less than an inch from her own. Its eyes were looking straight into hers as it bared its teeth at her.

"You ready to meet your fate?"

Lexi held her breath. If she had it in her, she would have pissed in the tub, but she did all she could to hold herself rigid and keep the demon's glare. She stayed quiet, keeping her attention fixed.

"ARE YOU?!" it bellowed, and the room shook. She could smell the death on its breath, and knew it was close to devouring her. Her life was in what she did next, and she had no clue what to do.

So, she continued to do nothing.

After a few moments, the creature smiled a wide smile and pulled itself back.

Lexi released the breath she had been holding.

"Hmm."

Then it was gone, and she slumped back into the tub briefly.

"Fuck this," she said to the empty room, though she had no clue if it was actually empty. She climbed out of the tub and reached to put back on her clothes.

To her surprise, they were gone. Instead, she found at the base of the fireplace a towel, and what looked like a set of clothes that matched what she had been wearing, except these weren't piss and shit stained. They looked new.

"What the ever-loving fuck is going on here?" she said. She was starting to think the demon had a thing for her.

Yeah, the monster that killed for fun and just threatened you while in the bathtub has a crush. Are you sure that's a good thing?

She wasn't sure, but at least she was still alive.

CHAPTER 24

The door had appeared shortly after Lexi was dressed. She hadn't noticed it at first. She finished pulling on the white cotton shirt that matched the one she had been wearing, and it was there like it had never left...

However, the poker and the ash shovel were gone. She had reached to pick up the gilded shaft of metal, only to find it was not where she had set it down.

Of course, Max wasn't going to leave her with a weapon. Or maybe he had. He had said that names weren't what she had expected. What else did she have wrong? She should go back to that library if it was still there and start reading more of those books.

But that was what Witchy Woman had done, and that hadn't helped her. How was reading more going to be any different for her?

She needed to figure out something.

She eased open the door, unsure what she would find on the other side. To her amazement, it wasn't the bathroom, but she was back in the hallway. She assumed it was the same one as before, as it looked identical. She was sure if she went to the door to her right, she would be back in the library.

Those books are not the answer. He wouldn't have them in there if they were. He wouldn't make it so obvious.

No, she needed to find his real office, not the one he had written in one of his books. She needed to find where he wrote. That's where she'd find anything of value. If there was some secret, he would have it there.

She stepped as lightly as she could as she made her way down the dark hallway. Other than the crackle of the burning candles, the house was silent. She made it to the next door and hesitated to reach for the knob.

"God dammit!" The shout was loud, and she quickly pulled her hand away and took an unconscious step back. The voice hadn't come from that door, but from further down the hall and she immediately recognized it as his.

Lexi held her breath. It was hard to place where the voice was coming from as the sound bounced around her. The hallway itself felt like it belonged in a maze, as it looked like it branched at the end, but just how large was this house? The hallway itself was massive, large enough that she could lie down in the center and not touch either wall. Then there was the ceiling that was twice as tall as she was. If this house had a second story, it had to be way up there.

Would she ever find a way out if she was looking for one?

With how the demon changed things around her, she didn't think she'd ever find the way, even if she wanted to.

Maybe that was what got the others killed. In the books, they were always focused on escaping, finding a way out. Maybe that was their fatal flaw.

Maybe that was why he hadn't killed her yet. Though she hadn't ruled out the horny demon theory.

"How could you let her touch me? What is wrong with you?"

Lexi heard the growl in response to Jacob's vitriol, but the writer seemed not to notice.

"She touched me. I don't like to be touched. She almost really hurt me, and you just stood there. I control you. How dare you? Why would you let her do that? She could have killed me."

Lexi felt like she was radioing in on where she heard the voices and while part of her wanted to get closer and watch Jacob argue with his demon, she knew how careless that was. It wasn't like she was going to get lucky and see the creature tear his head off. No, Jacob had something on the demon. She just needed to figure out what that was.

"Why?" She heard the low gravelly voice and could hear that lack of compassion.

"Why? What do you mean, why? I'm your master. You are bonded to me. You do as I say. You protect me."

The laughter that erupted and echoed around her was a surprise and she took another step back towards the other room. The malice that rode the waves of that laughter nearly collapsed her to her knees. She couldn't stop the chill that rippled through her bones and left her momentarily feeling as though she would never again know warmth.

"Why would I protect you? When did I ever give you that misconception? I serve your whims so I can play. You bonded me to you, yes, but your death only releases that bond. Don't fool yourself into thinking I am your protector. I look forward to your demise and will enjoy it such as I have enjoyed all my playthings."

A silence fell in the hallway, and she could imagine the fear and realization that Jacob was feeling.

"But what about the other? You- you've protected me before."

"Earthly law. That tribal deception. Those we had bargained for. Those are mere parlor tricks. You are under no mortal protections from us."

"But-"

"Enough of this. There are ears listening."

Lexi had been working her way back to the Witchy Woman room and quickly dashed inside.

"Fuck," she hissed to herself. She didn't have long. The bastard sold her out, after all. Fuck-fuck, what was she going to do?

Think, that's what you need to do. Think!

Well, when did the demon start showing up in Jacob's books? You know his books better than anyone. You know when they were published. When did Max first show up?

Lexi's mind raced as she worked her way through his catalog and laughed when she realized the answer. It was so damn obvious she was damn near right on top of it.

Witchy Woman.

It wasn't his first book about murder and mayhem, but the books did shift after Witchy. Something inside her said he was killing people long before Max got involved. Maybe that is what drew Max to him, but the carnage was there long before that first summoning.

She could be wrong, though. Maybe he had started out as an excellent writer. There were so many out there unnoticed, maybe he got frustrated, saw the deal and took it. Maybe he wasn't always the psycho, but who was to say? You're only remembered for your latest horrific action. He could have been on par with Mother Theresa, but for all that, he would always be the murderous bastard getting ready to kill her.

Focus.

Witchy Woman.

What could be the link? What was binding the demon to Jacob?

Lexi scanned the room, trying to focus, when something crashed into the wall behind her. It didn't open, somehow the lock holding it in place, but that meant she didn't have much time. She needed to find whatever it was, and she needed to find it now.

"Well, isn't this a surprise?" Jacob said from behind the bookcase, talking through the door. "Here, I thought you were dead. I have your friend. We'll have to take you back to her. Just open this door."

"You really need to work on that sales pitch."

"Open the door."

"Doesn't matter. You unlock that door, I'll run into the circle. Protection circles work both ways." She had no clue if that was true or not, but she did know it wouldn't matter. She knew the circle was broken, but Jacob didn't know she knew.

What can I do with that information? She wasn't sure yet but was trying to formulate a plan. She needed to stay focused on finding the binding agent but had to stall Jacob for as long as she could.

"Max is with your friend. I told him to play. The longer you're keeping me out here, the longer he gets to do what he does best. He's a demon, Sydney. He's from hell. He knows how to torture people really well, and he's good at it. I can only imagine the things he is doing to her right now."

Lexi looked around the room, taking note of her options. She thought she might have something; it was something she had almost forgotten about Witchy Woman. It wasn't a part of the plot, but had been early in the book. She doubted it was ever supposed to be a part of the story, as it was a red herring to the rest of the novel.

But would it work?

"Have you seen him in snake form? He loves to penetrate innocent characters like that. He has such a thing for phallic symbols.

"I've seen him torture characters for weeks. He's almost stretched it out for a full month one time. Not all my characters make it into my books. There are some that are just boring and just sit there and cry.

"I thought you were going to be one of those characters. You really surprised me. I have to say, I'm impressed. The house must have liked you to allow you to escape. I wonder why.

"Doesn't matter. You have found yourself back to being my main character. Now your friend is just the sidepiece. I can't even remember her name. Oh yes, I can. She was Sydney. I guess that had made you Drew, but that doesn't fit anymore, does it? What should we call you...?

"I'm thinking Joanne. It's not a great name but I can't really call you John even though you have the Die Hard vibes. So, Joanne, for now, until I come up with something better.

"Hey, you're a super fan of my work. How did it feel to be one of the main characters? You actually get on the inside and see how I write. You know, every interview I do, they always ask me how I come up with the idea for my books. You are getting an inside peek. You are the story."

Jacob finally stopped talking, and she held her breath, trying to hear what he was up to. She held it until she couldn't hold it anymore.

"Not yet. He can't get in here. Not yet," Lexi whispered to herself, her hands shaking as she tried to work the matches in her hand. She had dropped a few on the floor but focused on the ones remaining in the box.

"Open this door, Joanne. Open it right now!" he yelled, and she could hear his anger. He had tried so hard to be sweet moments ago, but she knew it was coming. Jacob struck her as a mommy's boy always used to getting his way. He didn't like that she wasn't giving into him.

"Fine. Even if the house won't open the door for me, I just need to go back to my office. I have the key. I am coming in there."

"Whatever, asshole," Lexi said, taking a sigh of relief. She had options. She could escape through the tunnel again if she wanted. She was sure there were other options as well, not that she had time to figure them out.

* * * *

There was still the smell of smoke in the air when she heard the key in the tumbler as it turned. If she was going to do this, now was the time. She had the book, the one she recalled from earlier on the shelf. She was in the circle and surrounding her were candles burning on each of the points of the pentagon.

She started chanting as the door opened.

"Ad te proficiscar, canis psychotici filius. Ad te proficiscar, canis psychotici filius. Ad te proficiscar, canis psychotici filius."

"Get the fuck away from there."

She ignored him, continuing to chant. She could feel a breeze on the back of her head, but paid it no mind, closing her eyes so she could focus on the words. She spoke them, the lines back-to-back, each time getting louder as she did, putting more anger and hate into the words. She poured all her frustration, her hurts and her pains, all the aches that racked through her body.

"What do you think you're doing? Are you trying to call Max? You never will."

"Mackilemdrux. Mackilemdrux. Mackilemdrux. Ad te proficiscar, canis psychotici filius Jacob Skulz."

The wind picked up in the room and she could feel the demon's presence. She knew it was there as the warm breath erupted on her neck.

She had a brief moment of fear clutch at her chest as she was sure he was going to realize what she had done. She wasn't ready yet. No, it can't know. Not yet. She needed more time.

"Stop this. I command that you stop this," Jacob said to her, and she had to stop from laughing when he actually stomped his foot down like an overgrown child.

She had to see this through. She had to do this, or she was dead.

"Adiuva me occidere eum. Adiuva me," she continued to chant. Behind her, she could hear the low, rumbling growl and felt something gripping her shoulder. She looked and saw the large, clawed hand grab her, its talons tightening, cutting through the shirt and into her flesh.

"Stop!" Jacob yelled again, and she saw him take a timid step forward, but quickly backed away, looking at her with fury bulging in those eyes. He hated her. He would tear her apart if he could, but he was too scared to get any closer.

"Qui te magis occidere vis. Me vel illum."

Suddenly, the book fluttered in her hands, flipping back and forth through the pages. She had no clue what it was looking for, but she heard its growling voice.

"Sacrificium."

The book was still in her arms, and she looked at where it had stopped. It took her a moment to scan the page. She just had time to find it before the book flew from her hands.

Then the demon had her gripped by both shoulders as it ripped her from the circle.

CHAPTER 25

Lexi recognized the room the moment the door opened, though she took notice that the chair she had initially been bonded to was gone, replaced by a mess of blood and hair that was in the shape of a body. It was one she was pretty sure she already knew.

She barely had time to see her friend before she was thrust hard, aimed to land on top of her.

Lexi fell but did her best to reach out, trying not to land with her full weight on Amanda. The pool of blood that surrounded her friend turned Lexi's stomach, and she tried not to focus on it. Instead, she channeled that anger toward the man that was following her into the room. She couldn't see Max. The demon had gone back to being invisible once he had launched her in the room, but she could sure as hell see the smirking writer as he sauntered in.

"Looks like Max did a number on your friend there. Is she even alive? That is an awful lot of blood."

Lexi pulled back Amanda's hair to see if her friend was breathing when she felt the faint rise and fall of her chest as it rubbed against Lexi's

"Ame. A- are you okay?" Lexi said. She was having to fight back the tears. She was able to get the hair away from Amanda's face, and Lexi gasped, recoiling from what she saw.

Amanda's remaining eye was open and looking up at Lexi, though from the glossiness, Lexi doubted she even saw her. The other eye was destroyed. It had ruptured in a fountain of goo that was streaked down the collapsed right side of her face. Her mouth was gone, ripped flesh that had been torn away so only teeth were visible. They were twisted in a grotesque smile that was done to her, and not one of nature.

Amanda had her ears, though. They were completely untouched, probably left so she could hear her own screams, or so that she could hear Lexi once she had made it there. Lexi wasn't sure, but it was one of the few areas left that was not bleeding.

Max did this to her. Max had torn her apart like this, had used her as one of his playthings. Amanda didn't have a chance once Jacob had let him loose on her. Max had come in there and tore her apart piece by piece.

Max had done it, but Jacob had ordered it.

That burning grew hotter in Lexi's chest as she remembered how it had been Jacob who had told Max to come in there, to torture her friend.

Damn him. Damn, she wanted to do this to him. She wanted to tear him apart piece by piece. He should get to know what it felt like. He should truly get to know what one of his characters goes through.

"Is she still alive? Max, you didn't kill her, did you? You know, I wanted to see her die. Come on."

Lexi's hands clenched into fists as she turned to glare at Jacob.

"You fucking bastard."

Jacob looked at her, and she wasn't sure what he saw, but he took a step back toward the door.

"Max?" Jacob called out.

Lexi started to rise. She was so angry, the rage rising up, burning inside her, that she needed to unleash it. She was ready. She was fury incarnate ready to rip this man to shreds with her own bare hands.

She stopped when she felt a light touch on her hand. Lexi looked down to see that Amanda was trying to reach out to her. Her hand was trembling with the effort as she struggled to lift it.

Tears touched the corners of Lexi's eyes as she saw what was left of her friend's hand. The skin and muscle had been peeled back on two of her fingers and she could see the slivers hanging. He had peeled back the skin in little strips, doing so individually. Then there were the exposed bones, broken in multiple places, as if skinning hadn't been enough for the fucking bastard.

It looked like he was about to start on the third finger, her pointer finger, but had stopped at just the first strip. A single piece of flesh hung as it was trying to grab her arm. The mess of what was left of her hand streaking blood down Lexi's arm.

Lexi's jaw clenched, hard, and she had to close her eyes to bite down the anger and pain that was rolling through in a thunderstorm of emotions.

There was a noise coming from Amanda. Lexi took a breath, trying to calm herself to a place where she could open her eyes and not immediately rush Jacob as every part of her, every fiber, wanted to tear into him.

She opened her eyes and looked at her friend. What was left of Amanda's mouth was moving, and it took a moment for Lexi to realize the noise she heard was Amanda trying to talk. It looked painful, as her friend fought harder to mouth something.

Lexi lowered herself, putting her ear to Amanda's face, trying not to show her level of repulsion.

Amanda struggled to repeat herself a few times, and Lexi tried to understand her. When she did, she looked down at her friend in shock.

She watched again as her friend worked to mouth the words, "Kill me."

That was it. Lexi felt the snap, the final straw, so to say, strip away from her mortal being, and she screamed. She roared with a primal rage that erupted from her core, all that tension and hate that had been building up inside her, pushing for release.

She rushed at Jacob. Hurtling herself with all her fury propelling her, giving her the strength of abused and tortured woman everywhere as she went to slam into him. She put everything she had into rushing forward, leaning into it as her arms were raised and braced to slam into him and push him back against the door. She committed all of herself, every ounce of passion that had been exhausted out of her, that she had regained in the last few hours. All of it...

Only to feel like she slammed into a brick wall, invisible, blocking her way. She was inches from hitting him and clawing his eyes out.

Jacob stood there, stunned. She could see that he had braced himself, expecting the blow. She saw the fear that had created a dark spot on the front of his pants. His mouth opened that little bit, the shock that she saw slowly creep its way back into that smirk she had grown to hate.

That was as much as she saw before Lexi was ripped away from him. She went flying across the room, thrown into the pile of bones that had hidden her escape before. Out of the corner of her eye, she saw that the hole was gone as she crashed into the bones spread around it. They erupted in a shower of cartilage as they rattled away, and she felt the wound in her side rip open.

A whimper of pain escaped her lips, no matter how hard she struggled to hold it in. Her side flamed like it was on fire and she could feel the wetness already soaking into the shirt.

"Oh boy, that was close. Thank you, Max, that was a close one, and boy, I gotta say, you really did a number on Ms. Drew here. Or are you, Sydney? I'm going to have a hell of a time keeping these names straight in the second draft."

Lexi breathed shallow as every breath felt like knives stabbing her.

No, it wasn't going to end like this. She had been there before; she was not going back to this. Never again.

She reached out and braced herself, shifting so she could roll over. She rocked back and forth to give herself the momentum she needed as she struggled to work through the pain.

She made it to her hands and knees and kept moving, not allowing herself to rest. She put her hand on her knee, using it to continue her journey up. She stopped when she saw the bone covered in blood. It had been the one to stab her. Looking at the red tipped bone, she saw it was in a T-shape that ended with a sharp edge. It looked like it was carved and designed to stab someone. She reached out and grabbed it before pushing herself up.

"You are a tough one. I think this book is going to be a lot of fun. You know, I'm only in the first couple of chapters. I was worried I was going to scrap it. I'm so glad I didn't hit that delete key."

"You're going to wish you had," she gasped, struggling to pull in another breath as she stood and looked at him. "You're gonna wish you had taken someone else. I'll make sure of that," she said as she held the bone, positioning it so the six inches of bone protruded through fingers.

"Of course. Hey, Max, why don't you take her friend over to her, show her what she's in for?"

Lexi couldn't see Max, but watched as Amanda was made to look like a marionette on strings and was lifted so she was floating in the air. Her toes barely touched the cement floor, her head to her chest, lost in her hair. She reminded Lexi vaguely of the girl from that Ring movie until Amanda started to move closer to her, her toes dragging on the floor.

Lexi took a step away from the approaching girl, trying to use the wall to her left to get around it and make her way to Jacob, who stood there by the door. He continued to watch her, and she wanted to take this bone and ram it down that smug smirk and pound it deep into his throat. He needed to choke on it like he needed to choke on his own words. Then she was ready to break both hands for the words he typed, the people he tortured to write them.

An unseen force pushed her back to the corner and turned her to watch as her friend neared.

Lexi adjusted her grip on her bone, drumming her fingers as she held it, feeling the time was coming. She had to get this right. She needed to do this. She'd hoped there was another way. This was not how she wanted this to go. Amanda had come there to save her, to find her and get her out of there. Lexi wished she could do the same for her friend.

A piece of flesh dropped from Amanda's hand, and Lexi saw as part of the ichor that had once been an eye dripped from her hair. She wasn't moving, not on her own. Was there anything left of her?

Amanda was only inches away from her when she stopped, and Lexi saw the little movement in her chest indicating she was still breathing.

She felt the tear rolling down her cheek as she closed her eyes. She had to do this. It was the only way.

Yeah, and years from now, is that still going to be the lie you tell yourself? She doubted she would care by then. She saw Jacob; she knew her future.

"Max, why don't you kill your plaything? Do it nice and slow in front of her," Jacob said. The matter-of-fact tone of his voice helped strengthen Lexi's resolve.

"Makelux, I bind thee to me," Lexi said through her gritted teeth.

"What are you doing? You can't do that. He's bound to me. I don't release him," Jacob shrieked from the other side of the room. He took a step towards them but then looked to the demon and the woman it held.

Did he realize the demon was making no motion to do his bidding? Did he see his world crashing down around him? Was he that self-aware of reality, or had he truly fallen into believing his own books?

"Makelux, I bind thee to me." Her jaw loosened as she felt a warmth flooding her, steeling her veins. Her resolve strengthened. She was doing this, and she was going to make that asshole pay.

She only wished that there was some other way for this ritual to end.

Darkness flowed into the room like smoke erupting from the vents, but no, this came from everywhere. It swirled around them as if driven by a gale of wind. It blew her hair and made it hard to breathe and speak.

"With this sacrifice, your will be mine. Makelux, I bind thee to me," she shouted, the darkness having spread so thick that she had no way of seeing the writer until he appeared just inches from her. He slammed into her, and the bone shard flew from her hand. It disappeared from her sight as she struggled to push the larger man off of her.

"You bitch!"

A claw slashed out of the darkness. Lexi barely saw it in time and shifted to her side. It missed her but caught her shirt, the fabric shredded into strips. The writer hadn't been so lucky, and those talons caught him in the shoulder.

He cried out in pain, grabbing at the ripped flesh as blood flowed freely. He looked at her in horror before scanning the room. She wasn't sure what he was looking for, as she was not able to see anything. Finally, he turned back to face her.

"What did you do?" he said to her. "You released him, didn't you?"

She smiled, right before her fist connected with his face.

A lightning bolt of pain shot through her arm, but it was worth it as his face fell back, disappearing into the dark.

She didn't wait. She quickly dropped down. She needed to find that bone shard before he came back. She had to finish this. Jacob was right. She had released the demon, and they had a deal in place. It was only their deal that kept it from tearing her to shreds, doing what it had to Amanda. She had to finish the binding ritual before they were all dead.

There were so many bones, but none of them like the long, sharp bone she was looking for. It wasn't the bone that was important, but she needed to know it could do the job. She wanted it to be over with as quick and as painless as possible.

She wrapped her fingers around something she couldn't see and felt a tingle run through her. She had it. She didn't need to see it to know. She just did. She grabbed it and stood, turning back to face her friend who was still visible, the darkness swirling around them, but right there, they had a clearing.

It was time to do it. No more stalling.

"With this sacrifice, your will be mine. Makelux, I bind thee to me."

Lexi slammed the bone straight into Amanda's chest, pushing with all the force that she could. She had to, if she was ever to burst through her friend's breastbone and into her heart.

She prayed that Amanda would forgive her as she made her best friend the sacrifice she needed to complete the ritual.

CHAPTER 26

Lexi didn't have much time. She knew it. Jacob just left the door to get the key to get in. She thought she had figured it out, but she needed to be quick if she was ever going to make it work.

In Witchy Woman, there had been an incantation that she'd used, but it didn't work because she used the wrong one to bind the demon. The one she used was one of two that she had found. One required a sacrifice, the other should have worked without. Later in the book, the reader found out that to bind a demon it always requires a life.

What was important was the next part. The binding only lasted as long as a portion of the sacrifice was preserved.

It had been weighing on Lexi as to why Jacob had kept the head. She had written it off as Jacob being a collector, and she was sure if she searched more of the house, she would find other trinkets of his conquests. He probably had a whole room dedicated to items, or maybe even body parts from those that died to be a part of his books.

This one had felt different, though. It wasn't on display or with any other trophies. It was in a room that felt abandoned. She doubted he had ever stepped foot in it since the initial ritual. This didn't feel like he was collecting it. No, he was hiding this one, and if he was hiding it, there had to be a reason for it.

She opened the drawer, and those lifeless eyes looked up at her, the fear preserved in its horrified state.

"I can only imagine how betrayed you felt. You thought you had won. You had channeled the demon. You were making your escape. You had no way of knowing you were being lured into a trap."

Lexi pulled the head out of the drawer, surprised by its weight, and set it on the floor behind the desk. Now she just needed to find a way to burn it and hope that it would burn fast enough before Jacob came back with the key. She had no idea how long it would take him. Would he hurry?

No, he'd take his time. He loved drawing things out. He was a writer. For him, it was always about building up that tension, playing with side plots or cliffhangers between chapters. All those damn writing tricks that always pissed readers off.

Fuck him!

That didn't matter to her. She still needed to hurry. She couldn't let him stop her.

She went back to the desk. She'd searched the top drawer before and hadn't seen anything. Still, she opened it before she could catch herself and had to stop, her mind trying to catch up to what she saw. There was still the junk from earlier, the now empty flask, the other random crap, but now on top of all of it was a box of matches and a little yellow container of lighter fluid.

She couldn't keep her jaw from trying to hit the floor. She sure as hell knew that hadn't been in there before. Was the house helping her? Was it the demon? The demon had a thing for her, or so it seemed, earlier. She wasn't sure why. Part of her didn't want to question it, but still it nagged at her.

Was she doing the right thing? If she did this, this would be unleashing the creature to kill them. That was, unless she could banish it.

Lexi stood over the head, looking down at those lifeless eyes as her mind raced. Was there another option? Could she banish the demon? That had to be an option. There had to be a way to do it, but could she find the incantation in time? There were so many books, and what if she got it wrong? Those eyes looking up at her were a stark reminder of what happened if she did.

Could she trust anything she found in any of the books in there?

She looked at the lighter fluid in her hands. The house would only show her what it wanted her to see. Would it only give her what it wanted? Did it want the demon on the loose or banished?

Her gut told her the two were used to each other and that the house was partially controlled by the demon.

Nothing could be trusted. As if to confirm this, she saw a book on the corner of the desk. It wasn't a spell book, or anything that could help her, but it also wasn't there before. It was a translator's guide for Latin.

Who the hell speaks Latin?

She felt the room get warmer and the hair on her neck rose.

"Max?"

A low grinding chuckle rumbled.

"What are you going to do to me?"

"I haven't decided yet," the naked demon growled as he appeared standing next to her, looking down at the head. She could see him sneering at it like he wanted to be the one to burn it.

"If I release you, you're going to kill me."

"I could kill you now. Nothing's stopping me."

"No, Jacob doesn't have some command to keep me alive for his story."

"He wants a story. Your life doesn't matter."

Lexi stood there and, even in the growing heat of the room, felt a chill.

"Why haven't you?"

The demon just harrumphed at her and met her eyes, its red eyes glaring. He was challenging her. Was she smart enough to figure it out? She sensed that her life depended on her next move.

"You want to make a new deal? What's wrong with your current one? Other than you killing me, which is something I don't want you to do."

The demon didn't answer her, but nodded in the affirmative.

He wants a new deal. What did she have that he could want? He loves killing. What else do demons want? Demons... hell, so sinners. Hell wants sinners, right, punish for the sin, but did that apply up here? Sinners go to hell, but he was freed from there. Were sinners still the goal?

What if they were and Jacob wasn't delivering?

"You like killing and torture. Does the victim have anything to do with it? Do you get anything out of that?"

The demon shook his head and snarled at her.

"Do you not get anything out of that, or the victim doesn't matter?"

The demon growled his response, showing more of those sharp, pointed teeth as he continued to snarl.

This demon was angry, and she felt that anger focused in her direction. It wasn't for her though, but was channeled toward her, frustrated at her inability to figure out what it wanted.

"It doesn't matter if it's me or someone else. It doesn't matter who the victims are. You're just pissed that asshole was the one to bind you. You want revenge, and you want someone to channel that and direct you in that revenge.

"You like being ordered around. You just can't stand him. Is that it?"

The demon's glare didn't change.

"Okay... okay, here's the deal. I'll bind you, then we will get him. Once he's dead, you'll still be bound to me and you're going to do for me what you did for him. I will become an influencer, and I will be Flix famous, and everyone will listen to my every word like its gospel itself."

The demon nodded. Lexi started coating the head beneath her in the lighter fluid.

"Your friend is nearly dead. He will be back soon. Read," Max said as she let the match fall. She quickly stepped back as the head caught in an instant blaze and began burning faster than she would have imagined.

She looked at the book on the desk. Max was gone, but she saw the sheet of paper with a series of words in it. She had no clue of the meaning but quickly started to look them up as she strolled back to the summoning circle, knowing the writer would be back soon.

After looking up each of the words, she laughed. Max had a sense of humor, or so it seemed, as he wrote out exactly what he wanted her to say to that asshole.

She heard the key go into the lock. She looked to the head to see only ash left on the floor. Around her there were now candles lit to cover up the smell.

Her stomach twisted as she realized what the demon had said. Amanda was near death. Lexi didn't have much time left if she was going to save her.

CHAPTER 27

Lexi watched the body of what had once been her best friend fall to the cement floor. Lexi had seen the life fade from her. Then Max released his grip, and she just fell. There was nothing left to keep her upright. Just like that, she was gone.

Lexi was still processing what she had done, the blood still on her hands, when the air in the room shifted. The dark clouds were no longer swirling around the room as their vortex had changed. They were getting closer, tightening around her. As they picked up speed, she could feel her hair being tossed about while she was lifted up by the whirlwind.

As it focused on her, she could feel the fire that burned beneath the wind. It was the hate, the anger, the pain of an underworld forgotten by heaven after it had been cast out. She could feel the screams of a million men as their endless tortures were forged in the fiery pits below.

It consumed her, and as she breathed; she saw the darkness racing to fill her lungs. It burned with each breath, but she found something strange as it washed over her. It wasn't anything she expected as wave upon wave of sensation pummeled through her.

It felt good. It felt refreshing, like so many burdens and fears were suddenly lifted from her. It was freeing and intoxicating.

Then the swirling mass penetrated her. It swarmed into her open mouth, her ears, her nostrils. She saw as strands were racing through her fingertips, burrowing under her fingernails. It was filling her from every direction.

She could feel the fire burning inside her chest; her fingers were flexing with the electricity of destruction. She ground her teeth as she wanted to scream but was not sure if it was in ecstasy or pain as it felt like every part of her wanted to lash out and take revenge on the world for what it had done to her.

Wave upon wave of darkness cascaded over her. The air around them whistled with the flow when she felt the change. It stopped forcing its way in. She wasn't fighting it. She wanted more of it. She could feel the currents inside her grow, and she was sucking it in, demanding more. It felt right, like it was a part of her, and she grabbed for it.

Behind her, she could hear the demon chuckling.

The room brightened as the last traces were like tendrils flowing into her. For a moment, her eyes went black as she absorbed the change. She wasn't sure what it was, but she could feel the demon now, his presence like an extension of her own.

She sensed that Jacob never had this level of connection to it. She had a brief flash of worry as to why that was, but a voice rumbled through her thoughts.

"He corrupted the ritual. You have not," was Max's answer, though he had spoken directly to her, his voice in her thoughts.

How had he known what she was thinking? Was he reading her mind? She looked at him, studying her. He glared back but then shifted into a smirk with a wink.

Fuck.

As the last of the dark ravaged her soul, she looked down at the body of her friend. Her dead friend, her best friend, lying there on the cement. Max had done that to her, but Jacob had desired it. Jacob had commanded it.

Lexi felt a thunderstorm of rage ready to erupt from inside her, but as she looked at her friend, she tried to feel sadness or remorse for ending her life. She thought about all the great conversations they had over the years; the fun times when they'd gone to the bookstore and spent the day talking books, or to the coffee shop where they would sit and make fun of their classes.

All those days were over. Amanda was gone, left to the pile of flesh that was at her feet. There was a bone pierced through her heart that Lexi had put there. Lexi had been the one to kill her.

So why couldn't she feel anything about that? All she felt was the rage, and when she tried to dig deeper, there was only this hole that was growing inside her.

It had taken that from her too, she realized. Was she even human anymore if she couldn't feel?

But she did feel. She felt a lot of things. She wanted to punish a lot of people.

She looked at Jacob. He had been on the ground when the darkness had flowed inside her, but once light filled the room, he raced to the door and was fumbling to get it open. His pants were soaked, and she could smell the stench of urine from where she stood across the room.

She couldn't stop the maniacal laugh that chorused from her as she watched him struggle. It wasn't even locked, he just had to pull it open, but the writer who had typed so many manuscripts that she loved couldn't use his hands. They were shaking so horribly that he couldn't grab it. They kept slamming into the metal and she watched as he was struggling with the pain as he fought to open it. Tears were streaking down his face and there was now a puddle beneath him as the piss kept flowing.

"Going somewhere, Jacob?" Lexi said, and she shocked herself at the sound of her voice. She could hear how the sex just oozed out her in a new sultry tone she didn't recognize. It was interesting, as she also heard how it was laced with a deep growl of violence at its edge.

She knew she should be upset, in tears over her friend, but she couldn't help but feel the strange euphoria at watching this man strain with just opening this door. She was going to have some fun with him, but not yet. She wanted him to struggle, to not be able to even figure out the door. He was so terrified he couldn't even get his own body to cooperate with him, and this was just the beginning. He was going to pay, not just for what he had done to her... he was going to pay for what he had done to all his victims.

Hell had come for him, and her name was Lexi.

The door finally flung open, and he didn't look back at her as he rushed to flee the room.

Lexi sauntered across the room, taking her time to reach the hallway. When she did, Jacob was a quarter of the way toward the other end. He was trying to run, but his legs seemed to fight him. He kept dropping to one knee, tripping over himself as though he couldn't remember how.

"Max, I think it's time to play, don't you?"

She could feel his presence but wasn't sure where he was. She thought he was behind the writer but couldn't be one hundred percent sure. She would have to figure that out, to know where he was. She wanted to make sure he was never anywhere he shouldn't be, like in the bathroom when she was trying to take a shower.

Even though she couldn't see him, she still knew he was nearby and was looking for her command to do what she wanted him to do.

"Max, sodomize him."

CHAPTER 28

Lexi watched the demon make itself visible as it was stalking behind the writer and saw as its large member hardened. Its twelve-inch-long cock with a girth wider than her fist rose, but then split into four distinct heads that looked like snakes with razor-sharp teeth. Each head snapped at the back of Jacob as he tried to run.

As the cock split, she saw it lengthen even farther, stretching out as the snakelike creatures chased after its prey.

The first head caught Jacob in his back, the teeth slicing through his shirt and caused a slash the width of his back. It sliced across and then started snipping, taking little chunks of flesh and fat.

Jacob cried out and tried to swat away the penis snake when the second head struck his hand. It bit down on the flesh, catching him between his thumb and pointer finger. It chomped down, but it did not let go. Jacob tried to pull his hand free, while the third head took snipping bites out of his arm.

Jacob could barely run now, fighting to get away from the penis snakes. His arm was pulled back behind him and the harder he tried to pull away, the more the trouser snake shook back and forth, fighting to hold on, tearing the muscle and flesh in his hand.

Then the fourth snake made a quick snapping attack at Jacob's Achilles heel. It first attacked his left, and Jacob nearly buckled. His knee threatened to give out, and Lexi wasn't sure how he was able to stay standing, let alone take another step as he did. It didn't matter though, as the snake made another quick, vicious attack. It shredded the right ankle, and Jacob crashed to the ground, all the snakes releasing him as he fell.

Landed, but didn't stop. He was bleeding from his various wounds, still trying to escape, though each time he tried to use his right hand, he crashed back to the red tile floor. He was slower, keeping the right hand to his chest, trying to crawl with just his left hand and his knee, but with his ankles bleeding, he wasn't moving very fast.

The snakes had merged back to becoming the demon's foot-long cock as it walked over the writer, its hooved feet on each side as Jacob still struggled to get away.

Max sliced down with his talons, cutting at the back of Jacob's pants. Lexi figured the demon was removing his pants, but the claws were long and sharp, and deep gashes ran from Jacobs's lower back down to the back of his thighs.

The pants were sliced in long strips and could easily have been torn away, but the demon was not pulling them off. Instead, it slashed down another strike, going in the opposite direction, cutting through more cloth. The jeans were in tatters and were falling away as Jacob kept crawling.

Though Jacob looked more like a toddler now, making his first attempt at creeping. He would try to climb back to his hands and knees but would collapse when he tried to use his legs or right hand. As the pants fell and the cut shirt slid to the side, the pale flesh beneath was already a bloody mess from the claw marks, but Lexi could see that bare ass in front of her.

"I'm not sure you're going to fit. That looks like an awfully small hole. Looks like it needs to be wider. Maybe we need to get him some lube," Lexi said, sauntering up to where Jacob had finally collapsed to the floor.

She was surprised as she found she was enjoying this. The hatred that burned inside her, seething with anger demanding to be expressed, was relishing watching the bastard squirm. She wanted this. She wanted more of this. Let the whole world burn, as she wanted to watch them all pay.

Her fingers twitched again, and she craved to get in on the action. She wanted claws of her own so that she could slice him herself. She wanted to tear into his flesh, to claw at him, to rip off one of his nipples like he had threatened her. She didn't want to just watch; she wanted to feel his blood on her fingertips.

Maybe this was why the demon chose to help her. Maybe he had seen this in her... maybe he knew her better than she knew herself?

She saw that the demon was staring back at her. She realized she was thinking of it less than a creature, but more as a 'him'. Was that the right word? He wasn't a man. From what she knew of demons, they didn't really have a gender, but could choose to be what they wanted. He obviously thought of himself as male.

She pushed those thoughts aside as she felt the hunger for blood rise inside of her. She had tasted so much of her own in the time she had been there, she wanted to taste his. She wanted more of his blood. He was not done bleeding.

"Don't you agree, Max? That hole needs to be wider, or you are never going to fit."

The demon nodded to her and bent down. He stuck one of his long talons into the sphincter of the writer and, with a casual flick, sliced through the back side of the man's ass. Jacob cried out, a high-pitched scream that the demon ignored but filled Lexi's stomach with excitement akin to racing down a high drop from a rollercoaster.

The demon waited patiently for the writer's screams to fade into more tears. The writer started to pound the tile as he reached out and pulled himself ever so slightly away.

The demon chuckled as he put his talon back into the hole and, in another flick, sliced the hole in the other direction.

Jacob's ass cheeks were becoming a bloody mess as the demon moved back behind him again. Its large member had gone soft but hardened as it positioned over the writer.

Jacob's tears were getting louder as he made another feeble attempt to pull himself away.

"Please don't. I'm sorry. I'm sorry. Please make him stop." Lexi barely heard the whispered voice as he had lost it, screaming.

"Oh, but Jacob, we can't stop. We have to finish the story. We wouldn't want your book to go unfinished, now, would we? Don't worry, I'll make sure it gets to your publisher," Lexi said.

The demon pulled Jacob back into position and then, without warning, slammed his rod through the enlarged cavity.

Lexi had thought he'd lost his voice, but the new scream echoed off the hallway walls as Jacob squealed.

Lexi could see that Max had only breached the sphincter and still had nearly a foot of cock ready to fuck Jacob's asshole, and already he was gasping for it to stop.

Max loved to torture, Lexi knew that, but she also realized just how much he was a master of it. He had stopped at just the penetration and waited for Jacob's screams to wane. He didn't wait for him to quit screaming, no, just for Jacob to begin to lose some of that initial shock from the large penis now engorged inside him.

Then Max forced in another few inches. He went hard and fast, slamming it in, catching Jacob completely off guard that more was coming. It gave the writer just that bit of hope that it was done, then, 'boom', another three inches filled him.

Jacob launched into another fit of screaming, and Lexi walked around them so she could look straight into his eyes. She lowered herself down, so that she was squatting in from of him. His face was wet with tears and blood was flowing freely from his nose. At some point, he must have convulsed so hard he'd hit it on the floor.

Jacob looked at her and mouthed the words, "Please stop him." To which Lexi smiled her reply as she rubbed her cheek with her middle finger.

"I think your publisher is going to love this twist. I mean, I'm sure she's felt that your books have gotten a little stale. It's always the same thing, a girl trapped somewhere, and bad things happen. Now we get to spice things up a little. We get to give it a huge cock in the ass."

Max forced himself in, much deeper this time, and Jacob spasmed. He shook violently, and blood exploded from his mouth. Lexi was close enough that some of it splattered onto her shirt and she looked at it.

"You know, Jacob, I think you're bleeding a little bit. You may want to see a doctor about that. Though maybe it has something to do with that cock in your ass.

"Cock in your ass. I just love saying it. Cock... in your ass. I mean, men always love talking about sticking it into the other hole, going into the back door. What's some other slang they have for it?

"Who cares? I just love the whole cock in your ass, and you know what? I think it's time for just that. It's time for that whole cock. Right, Max?"

Jacob had not relented on his screams, but as Max forced the cock deeper into Jacob's anal cavity, ripping him apart on the inside with his massive penis, the convulsing got worse. Jacob was bawling, coughing up blood as it erupted from him. His eyes rolled back in his head. His whole body was a mess, and she could hear him wheezing as he tried to breathe, struggling as though his lungs were filling with fluid.

"Okay, Max. Pop your load and give him a break. I'm not ready for him to die yet. Oh no, we're just getting started."

Max growled his approval as he continued to slam his penis into the writer, the demon working himself to climax.

CHAPTER 29

"Wakey, wakey, hand off snakey. You didn't think we were done, did you?"

Lexi gently slapped the sleeping writer, a quick succession of taps to wake him up. His face was covered in dried blood and had been resting on his chest.

"No, oh no. What did you always say, 'I'm the main character in your story?' Well, in case you didn't realize it, this is a revenge story, and I have a lot to be vengeful for. I'm not done with you yet."

Jacob wracked his head back and forth as though he were fighting to shake free the cobwebs of his thoughts. Though, as he drifted closer to consciousness, Lexi could tell the moment the pain registered, and he realized he was no longer on the floor.

His eyes shot open, and he looked wide eyed at Lexi, who smiled back at him.

"What was it you called me? Oh yes, Sydney, because you liked the Scream movies. Well, you know what, I liked them too. I also liked Saw, and well, I loved horror movies in general."

Jacob tried to pull himself up, but he struggled. He looked back and forth at his wrists. He was hung up on the wall, his arms and legs spread wide like a DaVinci pose as though he too was on display.

Lexi could see the horror registering in his face as he saw what was restraining him. Around his wrists wiggled what looked like a tongue that throbbed as it held his outstretched arm in place. The tongue creature wrapped around Jacob's wrist and disappeared through holes behind him, allowing it to keep him upright against whatever wall she was using. The creature had teeth to its underside, small ones, just enough to dig into his skin as it shifted with a rhythmic pulsating.

The writer looked at his other wrist to find the same disgusting creature, then he struggled to look down at his ankles. The things around his wrist tightened when he tried to pull away from them to look down.

"What the fuck?" he gasped, and blood drooled from his lips as he tried to speak. It led to another coughing fit and more of it erupting from him.

"Turns out Max can do all sorts of things with a little imagination. It's sad that you had so little of one, but hey, we can't all be some amazing horror writers. You know what they say, never... meet... your heroes." Lexi punctuated the last sentence by flicking Jacobs's nose with the back of a dart before she backed up roughly five feet from him.

"So, Mr. Writer-man. Are you ready to play a game?"

Jacob started crying again, not lifting his head, but his chest heaved with sobs.

Lexi threw her first dart, and it hit Jacob's chest. The metal tip made a small mark before falling to the floor.

"Well, what the hell?" she said as she stepped away. Max stepped up to where she had been standing and began to practice throwing with his own dart.

"Chest has a solid breastbone that can be hard to penetrate. You have to throw really hard to get through."

The demon threw his own dart that was larger and longer than Lexi's. It hit Jacob square in the center of his chest and pierced deep so that the entirety of the metal tip was stuck.

Jacob whimpered harder, but still kept his head bowed. Then Lexi smelled it and saw the brown streak of shit running down Jacob's leg. She couldn't help herself as she moved back to where she had been and aimed her dart. At first, she aimed again for his chest, but she was not Max. There was no way she was ever going to throw a dart through bone. She worked her way lower and threw.

She had been aiming for his penis, but the target was too small. Instead, she hit the large stomach that was sagging low.

"You know, Jakey, Amanda and I, our first love, was books. We would read and hang out together, just enjoying each other's company. We didn't go out much, but on the rare occasion when we did, we would go to this little bar just down the street from our favorite bookstore. It was on the opposite side of the strip, and while we'd never go there at night as it was a college town, during the day it was quiet. We could go there, have some sodas and play some darts. Amanda always kicked my ass, though she'd been playing for years.

"Amanda loved a good game of darts."

Lexi brought up her last dart, not giving Max his turn.

"You know, Max, we should really create a point system for this. The human dart board. How many points for an eye?" Lexi said over her shoulder to him. "Never mind. He'd have to look up first. Maybe I can try again and get his nuts."

Lexi walked forward until she was inches away from the man currently tied to the wall.

"I'd say hundred points per nut, right?" Lexi stabbed the dart hard into Jacob's exposed testicles.

Jacob's head rose, and he screamed. As he did, Lexi pulled out the dart and stabbed again, over and over, each time a reignited howl pierced her ears but died as it hit the sound dampening walls.

"Have you ever seen The Princess Bride? Or maybe you read the book? You're a book guy, you probably read the book. Well, do you know what 'to the pain' means?" Lexi asked once Jacob had quit screaming, and his chin rested back to his chest. At first, he didn't answer, and Lexi brought the dart back to his testes. She didn't stab him; she just rested the tip to the already bleeding sack of flesh.

"Do you know, 'to the pain'?" Lexi asked again, this time through gritted teeth.

Jacob nodded furiously.

"Good. Max, will you please start with his fingers? I want to wear his pinky on a necklace."

Lexi ran her finger across Jacob's chest, smearing the blood from the dart and pulling her finger away to lick it clean. She lifted Jacob's tear-smeared face and glared into his eyes when she heard the first crack and more of Jacob's screams.

"Good, Max. Keep going. Why don't you cut off his hand next?" Lexi said, not taking her eyes off Jacob.

Jacob shook his head frantically, but Lexi grabbed him, forcing him to keep his eyes locked on hers as he continued to scream. She could hear it as Max ripped off Jacob's hand and heard it plop to the ground behind them.

"So, Jacob, to refresh your memory, 'to the pain' means we are going to take your arms, then your legs, and while the Disney version didn't mention it, we're going to take your balls and then we're going to take your penis. Now in the movie they also took your mouth, but I'm going to save that for last. Do you want to know why?"

Lexi released her grip, and Jacob was quick to shake his head 'no.'

"Because I want to hear your scream. I want you to scream over and over. I want you to break your own vocal cords to the point that you go to scream and only a wisp of air comes out.

"You did that," Lexi said, pointing to where Amanda's body had fallen. "Max may have been the sword, but you were the coward that used him. You! You-!" Lexi struggled, trying to find words, but was at a loss. What she couldn't allow herself to feel in grief, she felt in anger and channeled it, grabbing Jacob's testicles and squeezing as hard as she could. She knew she promised to save them for last, but as the wave of fury hit, she didn't care if they ruptured right then in her hands. She just wanted to inflict pain. All the pain, as much as she could into and through this pig in front of her.

"Max, take his arm, but don't rip it off. Cut it right about here." Lexi indicated on her arm just above the biceps. "And make sure he doesn't bleed out. I don't want this to end too quickly. He's not ready for death yet."

Lexi leaned in close to the writer and whispered into his ear.

"To the pain."

Jacob screamed. She was unsure how much it would take, but she was determined to keep her promise. She was going to make sure he would never be able to utter another word. His voice was hoarse now, but that wasn't good enough. His vocal cords were going to break, and if not, she would rip them out herself.

CHAPTER 30

With no arms left to hold him up, Jacob dropped to the floor, a screaming fallen mass.

Lexi had barely enough time to get out of the way. After having Max break each one of Jacob's fingers on his other hand, then break the hand, there had been a tremendous build up until she had told Max to cut that arm as well. Both arms were cut away so that only nubs remained, and as the demon had used a sword made entirely of fire, the wounds had been cauterized with the slice.

Lexi stood over him, the screaming mass not even trying to get up. This was becoming too easy. They had broken his spirit, but there was so much more to his body to torment. They weren't done yet.

She kicked his side, her bare foot smashing into his ribs. He whimpered, but that was it.

"Get up!"

She kicked him again, but he still just rocked back and forth.

"Get up you loser. I'll make you a deal. I'll even give you a chance to live. You want to live, don't you?"

Jacob shook his head, but Lexi couldn't tell if he was shaking his head no or trying to nod.

"Go on. Run. This is your chance. You make it to the end of the hallway, and you can go. I'll not follow you; you're done. You make it to the end, you go, and I never want to see your ugly, fat face again."

This time, Lexi could tell he was nodding at her. As she watched him, she saw the nod grow to becoming more energetic as he tried to stand. Each time he used his nubs to push himself up, he crashed back to the floor, crying out in pain, but he kept trying. She saw that he was working himself to the wall and fighting through the agony.

At one point, the wounds must have burst open, as she saw blood gushing out from one of the nubs. He ignored it, sitting back on his knees, realizing that what he was doing wasn't working.

Jacob looked at her, and she relished the fear in his eyes. Oh, how she wanted to rush over to him right then and there to claw them out, but she forced a smile at him and did a little half wave, moving her fingers with just the slightest movement of her hand. It made her feel like a prom queen doing one of those flirty waves, but it was all a game, right? She was toying with him. Why not have a little fun while doing it?

Would she let him live if he made it to the end of the hallway...?

It didn't matter. He was never going to make it.

The shredded remains of his ass nearly touched the cement as he rocked back on his knees, trying to get his legs to work. He looked like he was trying to rock to one side and bring the leg around. He partially made it, but couldn't get his foot high enough. It drug across the floor. He lost his balance and fell to the side.

She watched as he flailed his nubs as he fell, his mind not understanding that there were no arms there to catch him.

He lay there motionless for a few seconds, and she thought she was going to have to walk over and kick him again. She started to take a step when he looked at her and tried again to push himself away. It was more of a flop away from her, but his second attempt was better as he rolled over onto his stomach before rolling again onto his knees.

"Oh, you got this. Just put some cheer into that spirit. You go, girl," Lexi said to him, trying to put as much pep as she could in her voice. It was hard, as all she wanted to do was take a hammer to his skull and be done with it.

He tried again; this time he was able to get his leg around as more blood dripped from the freshly reopened wounds in his ass. Then he rocked back and forth a few times before using that motion to push himself forward.

His legs immediately shook from the effort, still sore and in pain from how the fibers of muscle connected to his ass were now ripped to shreds. His knees buckled. He would have crashed back to the ground had he not fallen face first into the wall. He used it though and continued to push himself up, leaving streaks of blood, some from his pressing the nub that he tried to use to balance himself, and his freshly bleeding again nose.

"You are a bloody mess. Do I need to get you a wheelchair? Though I doubt you would want it. I'm sure I'd probably add a foot long peg for you to sit on. You liked to be pegged, don't you? You had a grand ol' time before. We had you squealing like a pig."

Jacob didn't look at her as he continued to use the wall to slide his way to the door.

"Oh, here, let me open that for you. Don't want you thinking I wasn't being fair in our deal."

Lexi walked around him, grinding her teeth to hold in her rage, being this close to him and not causing him some sort of pain. It would be so easy for her to push him down, make him have to work to get back up all over again.

The hardest fight was the struggle to hold it all back. She had come up with a plan. Sure, it was stolen a little from some other writers, one in particular, but what the hell, she wanted to perform an homage.

Lexi pulled open the door and stood there. He looked at her, that fear still etched in his eyes. Deep down, she believed he knew she wasn't going to let him live, but he had hope. That was what she gave him, and she couldn't wait to rip it away, just like she'd planned on ripping away those eyes.

She waited with bated breath for him to pass, making the moment he stood there just on the eve of the threshold stretch out for what felt like millennia. What was he waiting for? Was he trying to egg her on, to force her to give in to that rage? Did he know what she was going through, the dark desires running through her thoughts?

She didn't think so. She didn't see too many wheels turning behind those eyes as he seemed too desperate, craving only to make his escape.

No, he knew what was coming. He knew the moment he ran, Max was going to chase him down. That wasn't Lexi's plan, but that had to be what was going through his head as he stood there.

Lexi was caught off guard when he took off down the hall. At least, he attempted to. He only made it four wobbling steps before his legs gave out and he collapsed on the floor. She had expected him to get further, but it didn't matter.

Now it was her turn to play.

"Max, I need a hammer. Think Harley Quinn. What do they call those? Are they sledgehammers? That's it, right?"

"Harley Quinn uses a mallet, but for what you want, I believe a sledgehammer would be correct," the low voice rumbled behind her and a sledgehammer appeared, leaning against the wall. It's long, polished handle ending in a bright red, freshly painted metal block. It looked too nice and new of an instrument for the destruction she had in mind.

"That'll work," she said, and then she noticed the block of wood next to the metal hammer end. "Oh, Max, it's like you read my mind."

Lexi reached forward and grabbed the handle, pulling to lift it. With a grunt, she used the momentum of swinging it around to bring it up so that she held it in both hands across her body.

"That's heavier than I thought. I won't be able to use the block, but I think I can make this work," Lexi said, feeling the weight of it in her hands. It felt so heavy and real, like she could really do some damage if she decided to take it to an ex-girlfriend's car. That kinda thrilled her, the thought of having so much power that she directly controlled.

Lexi strolled forward, and it didn't take long before she was standing over the writer who was trying to find a way to crawl but not having any success. He reminded her more of a fish out of water than a man struggling to escape.

"You're pathetic. Just pathetic." Lexi kicked one foot and then his other, separating them.

"No," he whimpered, not taking his eyes off the end of the hallway. He was nowhere near making it. Lexi snickered, kicking him again, this time in his bloody ass that was a mass of torn flesh.

She pulled her foot back, covered in blood.

"Fuck. You're a mess."

Lexi readied the sledgehammer.

"So, Jacob, Mr. Writer-man, you ever watch Misery. I'm sure you have. Well, we are going to recreate the scene that everybody knows, but we're not going to do the book version. Yes, the book version is iconic, but the movie. The movie...it is just so visceral. How she brings down that sledgehammer-"

Lexi didn't need a board. She brought the hammer down, allowing gravity to add power to the blow as she slammed it to the tile floor. The tile shattered beneath the metal end, and it vibrated up her arms to her teeth. She dropped the hammer, unable to keep her grip.

"Fuck!" she screamed, trying to bite back the frustration and pain.

Jacob tried frantically to get away from her, though he was still more of a flailing bird with broken wings than a person trying to escape.

"Fuck you." She walked around to his side and forced him onto his back. He lay there looking up at her with those wide, terrified eyes.

She kicked him hard in the balls and watched as he writhed in pain as he tried to grab them. He rolled around, with arms that were no longer there, and Lexi dropped down, grabbing the balls and twisting them. She squeezed them in her palm, as she ground her teeth, trying to keep from screaming again.

"Ugh!" She let go and stood, grabbing the sledgehammer and, in one quick motion, lifted it and brought it down. This time, she made contact with Jacob's ankle. There was a sickening, satisfying crunch as she watched the ankle shatter beneath the blow, twisting his foot in an unnatural direction.

"There we go. See what I was saying? That sound, watching the writer's foot twist as she hobbles him. There are reasons why this scene resonates so well. It is the ultimate cringe. The sound of the bones just shattering," Lexi said as she brought down the sledgehammer onto his other ankle. Jacob hadn't quit screaming, and now his screams grew louder.

"Come on! Louder. I want you to rip out your own vocal cords while screaming. You can do it!"

Lexi brought the hammer again, this time on one of his knees. Without hesitation, though the exertion was tiring, she lifted the hammer and again brought it down on his other knee.

In mid-scream, his voice collapsed. She heard the pop and then, as hard as he tried, the only sound to escape him sounded like a wisp of air struggling to be heard.

She dropped the hammer behind him and knelt down between his legs.

"To the pain."

Jacob's eyes bulged as he tried to scream, and Max handed Lexi a freshly ripped-out scrotum into her hand. Blood ran through her fingers as she looked at it, turning it over to look at the unimpressive member. She thought she'd be more disgusted to hold a man's ripped out genitalia, but she found it oddly intoxicating.

Jacob was still trying to scream when she crammed it into his open mouth. He gagged on it as she continued to force it. He was going into convulsions again, trying to choke it out. He thrashed back and forth, trying to get onto his side, but she put her knee on his chest and then, with her nail-less fingers, pushed them into his eyes.

She wished she had nails to gouge them out, but blunt force would have to do as she forced them in until she felt them pop. The white viscous fluid oozed out from around her fingers with a satisfying sliminess that brought her back to days as a child, playing with toy slime. There was something about it that filled her with satisfying warmth as she rocked back to take in her handy work.

Jacob was still beneath her.

It was over. He was dead.

Lexi got up and walked back to the other room and to where her friend's body lay motionless on the floor. She plopped against the wall and pulled Amanda so that her head was against Lexi's chest.

The rage was finally calm inside her and the darkness gave way, letting the grief wash over her. Wave upon wave of it slammed into her and she felt the tears streaking down her face. She pulled Amanda tighter against her. She wanted to pull Amanda so tight against her that they became one, that Amanda would be back to life and there with her.

But it was never going to happen. Amanda was gone, and it was all because of her.

Lexi wasn't sure how long she sat there, but it didn't matter. She could get out of there now but knew she never would. Her life, like Amanda's, had ended in that room and she would always be back there.

She sat there as time passed. The writer may have been dead, but his story was still waiting to be told. She knew she would finish it. It was just something she felt like she had to do, but when it was done, he would finally be done.

In a way, he was lucky. His story was over. She had tortured his body, but the torture he had done would always be with her. Her story would never be over.

Lexi pulled Amanda tight to her chest again as she drifted off to the nightmares that would plague her for the rest of her life.

EPILOGUE

Hey Flix fam, LexiSexy here and I'm back again. I have a brand-new series of videos that I will be bringing with the help of a new friend.

I know I'm looking a little rough. That is because I am the recent survivor of being assaulted and tortured. Now don't worry about little ol' me. I survived, fought back, and no one will ever hear from that bastard ever again.

But there are women out there that don't get that. There are a lot of bad men out there that get away with murder.

Well, no more. We will not go back. So, this new segment is all about taking back control. Your body, my choice, right? Well, I choose revenge. So, we will be getting more of it. We will be going after bad actors on our way to one million followers, and thanks to my friend Max, everyone is going to watch. There is nothing you can do about it. You can try to scroll all you want; you will end up back here, just as the men will be.

So here we have our first 'guest'. Meet my new friend, Donald.

Donald here, is a rapist that like to grope woman and lie about it. Donald is a very bad man, and it's time that he gets what's coming to him.

Now you are going to see things on this page that you will want to unsee. These things need to be witnessed. We will not be blocked. We will not hit anymore glass ceilings or brick walls. We will succeed.

243

So, Donald, are you ready? Just to let you know, Donny, we are going to take your eyes, your nose. We are going to take every finger, then your arms, from the elbows, then from your shoulders. We are going to take your toes, your feet, your legs. We are going to take each nut individually and roast them. We are going to take your penis and cook it like a hotdog.

We will leave you with your mouth, though, and with your ears. We leave you as such, so as you feel every cut and every slice, you will be able to hear yourself scream. Max will make sure you stay alive as we take you piece by piece.

This is called 'to the pain' and we will watch every minute of it. Are you ready to start?

Yeah, well, we are.

Now viewers, this may get intense, but with every new guest, there is a certain way we like to begin.

And for everyone out there wanting to call the cops, don't bother. Thanks to Max, they'll never find us.

Now then, everyone ready?

Max... sodomize him.

AUTHORS NOTE:

So, if you've made it this far, I want to say thank you. This book was a huge experiment for me and one that really pushed me outside my comfort zone. I never like to put a lot of gratuitous situations in my books. It's just not my style.

That being said, I felt like after the 2024 election, there was some anger I needed to work through. Especially after the whole "your body, my choice" BS, I was blown away and so disgusted that it completely gave me a new focus on the direction of this book.

Initially, this book came from a road trip that I took. I was on my way to visit family when I had an order come in for a signed copy and wouldn't you know, it would be on my way to Illinois.

My first thought had been: Hey, I should message them and just drop it off on the way. It would kill two birds with one stone.

I allowed myself to think that for maybe fifteen seconds until I realized just how much of a creeper move that would be. Some random, strange guy who wrote a horror book message and says out of the blue to meet them? And because I would be just as scared of her as she might be of me, of course I would want a more public place... like maybe a department store.

I didn't do too much with the story then. I was more focused on my trip down and being with my family, whom I hadn't seen in years. However, while I'm down there, it seemed like everyone kept talking about the town the person was from. A nephew's football game was going to be there, someone just got a job there, the housing market there had taken a shit, it just never stopped. It's not even that large of a town, but it seemed like for that weekend it was the center of the world, so it kept the thoughts fresh about wanting to message that person and drop off their book.

So, on my five-hour trek back to Wisconsin, the idea came to me. Of course, the first thing I thought of was, with how popular a hashtag Book Mail was, how cool of an idea it would be to play on that.

Well, the first kidnapping didn't have much to do with the mail system, but it kinda did. I did feel like I had to justify it more, so I knew I had to add how Amanda was taken to be closer to actually giving out the address for some book mail.

In that five-hour drive, I pretty much had the initial story mentally plotted out. By the end of the weekend, I had the first few chapters...

I will admit this to me is my scariest book. That is to mean that I am terrified of releasing this book, as I never want any of you, my fans, to think that I would ever do anything like this. To me, a certain part of this book is breaking a sacred trust we've built in your orders over years, requesting signed copies.

However, at the same time, you bought this book because you wanted horror and to be scared. Well, may this book scare the hell out of the both of us.

As always, I hope you enjoyed and remember everyone... stay spooky!

Thank You,

Jason R. Davis

Special Thanks:

Alison Osborne
Marci Heath
Haley Singer
Davita Ferguson
Summer Jones
Shannon Michels

www.ingramcontent.com/pod-product-compliance
Ingram Content Group UK Ltd.
Pitfield, Milton Keynes, MK11 3LW, UK
UKHW011324220525
6046UKWH00026B/269